deep

down

popular

deep

down

popular

a novel by *phoebe stone*

ARTHUR A. LEVINE BOOKS
An Imprint of Scholastic Inc.

Very special thanks to Rachel Griffiths who worked on this book with me.
If you are lucky enough to have Rachel steering and cheering for you, you are lucky indeed.
Special thanks to Arthur Levine for his insightful dead-center suggestions and direction.
Love and thank you to dear Ethan and Kristy who read the book aloud to each other.
(And Kristy's mom too.) Thank you to Yvette and Bob for their help and to my mother
who listened over the telephone. And thank you to my husband, David, who is always there
in the middle of the night when I am full of doubt.

Library of Congress Cataloging-in-Publication Data

Stone, Phoebe, 1947–
Deep down popular / by Phoebe Stone. — 1st ed.   p. cm.

Summary: In a small, Virginia town, sixth-grader Jessie Lou Ferguson
has a crush on the hugely popular Conrad Parker Smith, and when he suddenly
develops a medical problem and the teacher asks Jessie Lou to help him, they
become friends, to her surprise.

ISBN 0-439-80245-8 [1. Coming of age — Fiction. 2. Popularity — Fiction.
3. Schools — Fiction. 4. Country life — Virginia — Fiction.
5. Family life — Virginia — Fiction. 6. Virginia — Fiction.] I. Title.

PZ7.S879De 2008   [Fic] — dc22   2007017198

ISBN-13: 978-0-439-80245-1
ISBN-10: 0-439-80245-8
12 11 10 9 8 7 6 5 4 3 2 1   08 09 10 11 12 13

Book design by Susan Schultz

First edition, March 2008
Printed in the U. S. A.   23

For my lovely
kind grandmother who
grew up in Virginia and told me
many stories about her childhood
there. Whenever she was upset,
she used to close her eyes and
say, "I'm going home
to Virginia."

I have to thank a big old shiny metal leg brace for my friendship with Conrad Parker Smith, and if I knew where that leg brace was today, I'd get my granddaddy to make me a nice wood frame for it and I'd hang it right up on the living room wall and every time I came downstairs, I'd look at it and I'd say, "Thank you. Thank you. Thank you."

I loved Conrad Parker Smith in the second grade. I loved him to the point where I used to hide in the bushes near the swing set on the playground at school, and when he'd go running by, I'd jump out and pull him down and give him a great big kiss on his cheek. He didn't seem to really mind, but he never kissed me back. I used to give up my turn on the swing so Conrad could ride just a little bit longer or my place in the lunch line so he'd be able to get some french fries before they ran out. I wasn't sure he even noticed me at all. Didn't even know if he knew my name. He had all kinds of girls chasing him around the playground. There was Elizabeth Parnell and Sarah Jane Peabody and Moon n' Stars Montgomery.

By the third and fourth grade we were a whole lot more proper. Nobody would have been caught dead kissing anybody. But in the beginning of fifth grade, Conrad Parker Smith seemed to have an unspoken reign over everybody. The girls all loved him (including myself). The boys really liked him, too. He was always the first to be picked for a soccer game or a baseball game. If a boy was looking for a place to sit in the cafeteria and Conrad had a spot open, you could be sure that boy would sit there.

For the most part, Conrad never paid that much attention to me, I imagine because I am what you call an *outdoors girl*. My mama calls me a tomboy, but I don't think I am. I'm just a whole lot happier when I'm running in a field or walking along a creek. Getting all dressed up is about the worst thing in the world to me. I hate sticking my feet in party shoes or wearing ironed party dresses. I about have to scream. Same thing with my hair. Right before we went downtown last year to get a family photograph taken, I hauled off with a nice big old pair of scissors and cut my hair practically down to the bone. My older sister, Melinda, has beautiful hair and it was all curled for the photograph and she was wearing a fluffy pink perfect cloud of a dress, and here I was in love with Conrad Parker Smith with my hair so short, you couldn't spit on it.

In second grade I covered Conrad with kisses whenever I could. In third I gave up my swing or my cookie or my bus seat coming home. By fifth grade I never said anything to him at all. I sat way at the back on the other side of the room getting As in spelling, spending a lot of time reading. I read everything on the accelerated reading list. I had stars all over my reading notebooks and stars on all my report cards and nobody I could really call a friend.

Meanwhile Conrad's popularity was growing. Not only did the whole fourth and fifth grade worship him but the big old sixth graders too, and all the little kids right down to the preschool bimbos. That boy's popularity was astounding, outstanding, overwhelming.

It was about six months ago, somewhere at the beginning of sixth grade, that something happened. Conrad's leg wasn't working right. He developed a limp that got worse and worse. His soccer game went downhill till he had to quit altogether. He found himself struggling to keep up on field trips. He started avoiding school dances and his popularity began to dwindle. It dwindled and it dwindled until the popular kids began to get used to not having him there at their dances and parties and soccer games. It dwindled and dwindled until the popular kids started forgetting to invite him altogether.

Then one day Conrad showed up at school wearing a big metal shiny brace on his leg. I wish you could have seen the look on the faces of the kids in that schoolroom. It was the worst possible thing that could have happened to Conrad's falling popularity. That leg brace put the final touches on Conrad's plunging status. Now more often than not, there'd be an empty chair next to him at lunch or you might even see him limping alone across the playground. The kids at Cabanash County Elementary have always been like the wind

running along the open fields around here, one minute high and sure and the next minute low and turned
away. Had I known! Had I known that leg brace would
be for me a kind of gateway, a door into a whole new
changeable world.

chapter 1

My see-you-later-when-I-feel-like-it friend, Elizabeth Parnell, has moved up to a table in the middle of our class so she can sit with Sarah Jane Peabody, leaving me back here all alone, bubbling and fuming like a pot of Mama's half-burned stew. Typical Elizabeth Parnell.

I am sitting here staring at a mess of a map, a big sloppy-looking thing the fifth graders painted of the United States of America. All the colors are mushed together so you can't even see our beautiful state of Virginia. It's just a blob of yellow lost in a bunch of greens and pinks. I'm sitting back here steaming and stewing 'cause that girl is about as reliable as a rubber raft with a hole in it floating backwards down the Cabanash River.

Our teacher looks out at our fourth-fifth-and-sixth-grade room like an explorer looking out at a new land ahead of her, like Lewis and Clark looking out off a cliff toward the empty expanse of America. "Jessie Lou," she says with her hand up over her eyes to shade the light so she can see way back to my seat in the far corner of the room under the big ugly kid-made map. "Jessie Lou?"

"Yes, ma'am," I say.

"Jessie Lou, don't you live over on Creek Road? Don't you live on the same road as Conrad Parker Smith?" she says.

I gulp. I take a swallow of classroom air and I gulp again. "Yes, ma'am, I do," I say.

"Well then, isn't that just perfect! The principal asked that somebody take the responsibility of helping Conrad Parker Smith to get his bicycle home from school. That bike's been here going on two months now," she says, smiling, "and I've been thinking he'll need someone to help him with his books, what with the new leg brace and all." She keeps looking at me with that Lewis-and-Clark hand up, shading her eyes, looking way out at the frontier, way out into the far-away world of the corner table.

I put my own hand up and brush it across the top of my head. I chopped my hair off real close last night so it probably looks like somebody buzzed my head with a Weedwacker. My hair feels all prickly and strange against my palm. "I'd like to ask you to be that person for the next couple of months," says our teacher.

I look down at my scrawny old legs that are covered with red scratches from the raspberry bushes. I was out last night scrounging around in the tall weeds trying to find a baseball that I threw too hard. My hands are all battered up, and I've got a mosquito bite on my knee that looks like a tarantula got after me. I take another swallow of that hard-to-breathe class-room air. "Me?" I say. "Me? You want me?" Then I roll my eyes over toward Conrad sitting on the other side of the room. He's shaking his head no and looking up at the ceiling in disbelief like there's something up there walking along on eight legs singing the national anthem.

"Yes, ma'am, I do mean you," says the teacher. "That'd be real nice and supportive." The room goes all silent like we're a bunch of strangers standing in an elevator together, that kind of uncomfortable silent silence.

"Okay?" says the teacher. She walks over to the chalkboard and goes on talking about Lewis and Clark and their expedition that we are studying. She writes *LEWIS* and *CLARK* in capital letters on the board. Then she writes out the name *Sacagawea*, the Indian girl guide. "Get out your history folders and let's think about a time when America was wild and undiscovered," she says. "When you got in a dangerous situation in the wilderness, you couldn't get on your cell phone to call your mama or your daddy. No, you were on your own. You had to rely on yourself."

I can hear my teacher's voice, but now her words are just a jumble of noise. I feel kind of shivering cold even though it's already roasting hot outside. My hands and feet feel cold. It isn't because my high-top sneakers are soaking wet 'cause they are dry today. It isn't because I stole one of my older sister Melinda's diet Jell-O pops from the fridge to eat on the way to school 'cause my granddaddy loves them so much he sucked up the last two this morning before anybody was awake.

I guess I'm freezing cold because I can't think of one word that I might say to Conrad Parker Smith. I can't believe my teacher would go and ask me, me of all people, to assist Conrad. I guess I could say, "May I help you?" but that sounds like I'm selling polyester blouses at Marlene's Fashion Barn on Route 28. The truth is, if I have to say anything more than yes and no, I'm sure I'll shatter into a million pieces and my granddaddy will have to come and pull me home in an old red wagon.

"Lewis and Clark were looking for a route to the sea. They were finding their way through the unknown. Imagine a sky at night completely dark with clean bright stars overhead. We never see a dark sky now — there are always lights of civilization on the horizon." Mrs. Duster looks up at the ceiling, her face full of wonder.

I look over at the table in the middle of the room where Elizabeth Parnell and Sarah Jane Peabody and Louise L. are sitting. They have little gold sticker stars all over their hair and they are hunched over together making fairy wands out of cardboard when they are supposed to be making some of the tools Lewis and Clark took with them on their expedition.

Sarah Jane Peabody is having a fairy tea party after school and she's got a pair of fairy wings in her backpack that she's going to wear on the bus riding home. Elizabeth Parnell left her fairy wings at home on her patio table by mistake so she'll be a fairy without wings at the party. I don't feel bad for her at all. I didn't even get invited. Maybe it's just as well. If I was to wear a pair of those wings, I'd probably look more like a sorry old housefly.

"Has anyone ever tried to find their way using the night stars as a guide? That's what Lewis and Clark did. They looked at the night sky," says our teacher, tilting her head back again and closing her eyes. Then she opens them and says, "Ever tried counting all the stars in the sky? You soon find out that it's a hopeless task. Isn't it."

Suddenly up out of nowhere the bell rings and it's lunchtime. I usually love the first Tuesday of every month 'cause it's Pizza Day, and here at Cabanash County Elementary you can choose your own toppings, and they'll heat it up for you all nice and cheesy and melty, and when you bite into that pizza, it's so tender and hot, you could just flap your way to heaven on a pair of old crow's wings.

Kids are pushing for the door now trying to get to that pizza, but I'm sitting here feeling faint like I can't move. Why did our teacher have to pick me? Does she know about all the poems I've written to Conrad? Does she know his smile sends waves through me like the waves knocking against the shore on the Cabanash River when a motorboat goes through? I don't think you can say no to a teacher if they ask you to do something for them. Can you? At least I never heard of anybody doing something like that.

I go out in the hall and kids start flowing around me like rising water. I am leaning against a mural created by a bunch of idiotic third graders who think cotton balls are just the greatest thing in the world and they've glued them all over everything, using them to make trees, bushes, even people's hair.

From here I can see Conrad Parker Smith up near the pencil sharpener, not hurrying to get to lunch like he used to. He used to be the first one at the pizza counter, smiling away and adjusting his invisible crown when everyone hurried over to get in line. Now I see him still sitting in class, one of the last kids to leave.

A little first grader has wandered into our room by mistake, and he's standing there next to Conrad's chair with his lunch box in one hand. The latch to the lunch box is half open, and while that little twerp stands there, all his wrapped-up sandwiches slide out on the floor. That's a first grader for you. They never seem to notice anything.

Conrad leans over and says, "Oh boy, now look what you went and did. What you got in here? Looks real good." He stuffs everything back in the lunch box. "Shoelaces are untied, too. Hey, you look like a disaster area. Where's your mama?" The little boy stands there looking up at Conrad.

I move away from the door and knock a couple of cotton balls off the mural by mistake. I'm just trying to stick them back on when Elizabeth Parnell and Sarah Jane Peabody walk by me in the hall, all cuddly with their arms tucked together. Sarah Jane already has on her nylon sparkling fairy wings. Elizabeth Parnell turns to me and smiles real sweet and looks real sincere and she says, "Y'all have yourself a real nice Pizza Day, Jessie Lou."

And I say, "Guess I'm not going to be here. I am going home for lunch."

It's one of those firecracker decisions that come up out of nowhere, a quick flash like a Roman candle on a hot July night. I gotta go home. Pizza or not. I just gotta gotta gotta go home.

chapter 2

I fly in the door at home and crash-land on that nice old prickly brown couch in the cool dark living room. I just love the way that couch kind of scratches the back of my neck and I can feel all the times I've sat here watching 1950s Zorro movies with my granddaddy. (Zorro is this guy who wears a black mask, who's a great sword fighter and always leaves the letter *Z* cut in a tree or a curtain when he's been there.) It's Granddaddy's favorite. Right now I need to think about better times, like last Halloween when Granddaddy dressed up as Zorro and took me trick-or-treating.

I can see the kitchen from here, and I stretch my feet all the way to the La-Z-Boy recliner and I close my eyes. Mama's whipping up a batch of chicken salad, and Granddaddy's hovering around nearby with two pieces of Pepperidge Farm white bread in his hands.

"Take more than your share, Granddaddy, it comes back to haunt you in the middle of the night," says Mama, tapping the side of the bowl with the wooden spoon and then washing it off in the sink.

"Well, if anything that looks like chicken salad comes knocking at my door tonight, I'll just tell it to go 'round and have it out with you first," says Granddaddy, laying some lettuce on his bread and then scooping up a bunch of chicken salad.

"Sew your own buttons on your trousers when you pop another pair then, Granddaddy," says Mama. "And while we're on the subject, I want y'all to get down in the cellar after lunch and haul up those bottles. Jean Duster's heading up another bottle drive this year."

"Well, sweetheart, not just this afternoon 'cause I'm going bird-watching," says my granddaddy.

"You mean you're taking your binoculars and you're gonna go poke around down at the construction site. Have you ever considered that the men working down there might not want some old geezer snooping around pretending to bird-watch?" says Mama.

"Well, it's a sad and sorry thing that's going on down there, isn't it, Jessie Lou?" Granddaddy says to me, poking his head through the kitchen door for a minute. "A miserable, rotten, terrible thing. That shopping mall is going to take all the business away from Main Street. And it will wipe out Bailey's Hardware, that's for sure."

"Those old Bailey brothers are stirring you up, Granddaddy. Far as I'm concerned, they're a couple of good-for-nothings," says Mama. "Wish you'd make friends with some of the seniors up at church. I don't think those Bailey brothers have set foot in a church for sixty years."

"People are magpies, honey," Granddaddy says, wrapping his arm around Mama's shoulder for a minute and then nodding his head at me. "I suppose they'd rather go over in their cars to that big flimsy shopping mall and get something that's going to fall apart but looks shiny and bright. Yeah, they're kin to magpies. Do you know what a magpie is, Jessie Lou?"

"Granddaddy," says Mama, "'course she knows what a magpie is — it's a bird, isn't it, honey? Shopping mall will be good for the town. People won't have to go to Charlottesville anymore."

"A magpie likes shiny things, brand-new things, things that glisten like a brand-new shopping mall. They don't care that in about ten years that thing's going to look like a box of rocks, Jessie Lou," says Granddaddy. "They just don't care."

My old granddaddy is practically obsessed with the new shopping mall being built. He rides over there with one of the Bailey brothers on a moped, and they poke around taking photographs of it and writing things down. Sometimes they go over there with their binoculars, whistling and trying to look casual.

Me, I don't really care about that shopping mall. I'm just sitting here thinking about Conrad and how I've loved that boy for all these years and I never in my life dreamed I'd ever have to actually talk to him. I close my eyes. I can just see him walking into the classroom this morning — the most beautiful, sweetest, full-of-brains boy I ever saw limping toward a table, pulling that new leg brace, dragging his books, wearing that tie-dyed T-shirt his mama made for him that says something about feng shui, which his mama is studying so she can get her life straightened out.

Granddaddy says, "I won't use that shopping mall. I'll go to Bailey's Hardware just like I always have. When I was young you could get an ice cream cone in there, you know that, Jessie Lou?"

"That shopping mall's gonna be real nice," says Mama. "The huge store over there is gonna be called Big Box Home and Hardware. Should have everything in the world, I imagine. Fifty-four different varieties of hammers and the like. You'll be just like a kid in a candy shop, Granddaddy."

Then Miss "Everybody's Favorite" (my older sister) comes primping up to the table. Every curl is lying there on her head like it is made out of plaster. She has an itty-bitty little ribbon in her hair and her finger-nails are all done up in pink. Everything about her is perfect, even her handwriting. She dots every *i* with a fat little perfect circle. She doesn't even bother to talk to me, especially now that I've gone and cut off all my hair so that my head looks like an old rug.

She moves through the kitchen nibbling a celery stick and then she comes into the living room and flops down into the La-Z-Boy recliner and calls out,

"Mama, did you sign that paper I gave you?" Then she puts her hands over her eyes and says, "Jessie Lou, your hair looks even worse than yesterday. What did you do to it? Mama, I gotta get back to school. Will you sign that paper?"

Granddaddy sits down next to me on the couch and sets a plate of chicken salad sandwiches on the coffee table in front of us. He has a can of Dr. Pepper soda with him. My granddaddy just loves Dr. Pepper. Mama says he doesn't have blood in his veins, he's got Dr. Pepper soda in there instead. "Well, sugar pie, have yourself a sandwich. Your mama made them and she's got the touch," he says, looking at me with his face all sweet and crinkly. "Well, I guess your hair does look like an old sheep-shorn throw rug. But you're still my little Jessie Lou, aren't you, sugar pie?"

"Jessie Lou, quit knocking your foot against my chair," says Melinda. "It's making me crazy."

I lean my head back against the prickly brown wool couch. It tickles my neck and I'm kind of feeling afternoon-lazy-sleepy. I wish I didn't have to go back to school for the rest of the day. I just can't stand the thought of having to say anything to Conrad. I don't know how anyone is expected to talk to somebody they've been in love with forever and a day. Especially me, the most unpopular girl in Cabanash County. I wish I could stay here and lie against this old brown couch forever and ever and ever.

chapter 3

About halfway back to school after lunch, I realize that I'm gonna be late. Realizing doesn't ever help. You can't do anything about it. Mama couldn't drive me 'cause she had to go back to Discount Beverage since her manager over there broke his right hand and can't run the cash register. "Honey," she said to me as I was picking up my backpack, "if he'd broken his left hand it would be different. But I gotta get over there pronto."

Nothing in the world is so quiet as when you're late. Suddenly there's nobody in the world but you and the sound of your breathing as you run. I don't see a car on the road. When I get to the parking lot, it's all full of sunlight and silence. The same with the playground. It's like everyone vanished from the earth, like something wonderful happened and I missed it, like everyone is somewhere else, and here where I am is the loneliest place in the world. And no matter what I do from now on, all afternoon that lonely late feeling is going to hover around me like a ghost.

My teacher doesn't make a move when I open the door and walk in. She doesn't pay me any mind at all but goes on talking about discoveries and discoverers. I pass Conrad's chair and I almost stumble, but I don't. Still, it sets off a series of muffled noises from the next table that sound to me like a bunch of ducks trapped in a box trying to get out.

"Has anyone noticed on the news on TV the space shuttle sitting on the launch pad at the Kennedy Space Center waiting to take off? Has anyone noticed that space shuttle is named the *Discovery*?" My teacher erases the chalkboard. "I want you all to make some kind of discovery yourself, and I want you to write me a two-page paper explaining that discovery. It will be due at the end of the year. Okay?"

"Even the fourth graders?" a kid calls out.

And Mrs. Duster says, "Yes, ma'am, even the fourth graders."

Seems everybody in Virginia is named Duster or Ferguson but they aren't related, or if they are, they don't know it. When my mama married a Ferguson (my daddy), she didn't even have to change her last name 'cause it was already Ferguson. And our school is full of Dusters and Fergusons. First names are a different matter. We have all manner of first names, but a few of the kids have hippies for parents. You can tell by their names, like Moon n' Stars Montgomery and her little sister, Sunflower. I think I'd feel half stupid to have a name like Moon n' Stars but I notice Conrad seems to think it's a pretty name 'cause he talks to her a lot and that just about burns a hole in my heart.

The last part of the afternoon, we end up drawing pictures of Lewis and Clark and Sacagawea and the wilderness that America once was. Quentin Duster, a little hippity-hoppity bean of a boy at the fourth-grade table near me, draws a great big dinosaur in his wilderness sticking its head up above the trees. Our teacher comes over and puts her hand on Quentin Duster's shoulder and says, "Quentin Duster, there weren't any dinosaurs in America during the time of Lewis and Clark. Those dinosaurs died out millions of years ago. Maybe you'd better start over and do a bear or a buffalo instead."

But Quentin Duster decides to draw in Clark with a boom box riding on the dinosaur's back. Our teacher takes a deep breath like she's doing some kind of special breathing exercises like that neighbor of ours who came over before she had her baby and practiced deep breathing with Mama while my sister, Melinda, held the stopwatch and timed everything.

I keep looking over at Conrad drawing quietly there at his table. I just have no idea how I am going to be able to help him with his bike. Why me? Why me? What am I gonna say to him? He has part of a smile stretched across his happy face, and I can only imagine what he's drawing but I know it's probably good. Conrad draws the best robots and space aliens of any boy in this class. And his space aliens aren't stiff and stupid-looking like some. His robots and space aliens always have faces full of expression and meaning.

Used to be when Conrad was drawing, there'd be several kids hanging over his shoulder like swamp trees hanging over the Cabanash River. But kids around here change. They change like the wind. They change like that river, one minute high and clear, the next minute all dark and muddy and low, leaving those cattails and swamp ferns standing there dry as a bone, all mucky and thirsty-looking.

When the bell rings, it's the loudest sound I've ever heard. The teacher starts rattling off which buses are where and who should line up in which line and when, and before you know it, the room has emptied out too quickly, like it was a recycling bin full of paper and somebody just dumped it outside into the wind.

And there's nobody left in here, not one single person except for me and Conrad. Conrad is gathering up a small pile of books and I pick up my backpack that suddenly won't zip closed and I kind of walk over to him and stand there like a stupid piece of furniture, like the time I was a chair in a Christmas play at church. Conrad doesn't say anything and I don't either. I pick up half his books and we kind of walk out of the room, me following him down the long dark endless hall.

At last we go through the double doors and the bright sun outside about kills my eyes. The soft heat of the air makes it hard to push on out into the schoolyard. I can see the bike stands from here, and I can see Conrad's blue bicycle sitting there just the way it has been for the last couple of months since Conrad's leg started to go bad.

If only I could think of a few words. Finally I come up with, "Oh, there it is." And those words just kind of fall through the hot, soft, full air. They seem to collapse onto the ground at my feet all broken and twisted. Conrad doesn't say anything and I kick those words aside, my face full of sun, just burning up.

Conrad doesn't exactly look at me. He's kind of turned away as he ties his books to the rack on the back with a bungee cord. Then I step forward and push the bike out of the schoolyard, and he walks along on the other side of it, his leg brace making a dragging sound as he pulls it along.

Out on the dirt road that follows the river I see water birds flying overhead calling to each other. The wind gets in the new leaves and makes a rushing rinsing sound. Spring gnats and bluebottle flies hover over the muddy slow water. Fish come to the surface making bubbles and ripples. I just keep pushing that bike, not stopping to rest, not stopping for anything.

Halfway home along the river, Conrad takes over pushing the bike for a minute, and while I'm swiping at the mosquitoes that are going after my head, Conrad kind of lunges forward into the tall grass along the river. I look up and see him plunging toward the bank, pushing the bike through a group of cattails and ferns. Then he shoves that bike down into the water. It falls forward and the current picks it up for a minute and then that bike sort of spins partway out into the river and comes to rest against a floating log, water pouring through the spokes and over the handlebars.

Conrad sits down in the reeds along the river. He drops like a dead weight and still he doesn't say a word. He just stares out at the water.

I stand here not knowing what to do. I look at Conrad's back down there hunched over in front of the water. I'm feeling so shy crows could just about pick me up and carry me away by my shoelaces. So shy I wish a whole screaming flock of them would drop me tangled in a big old lonesome tree somewhere else.

Suddenly I realize Conrad's books are on the back of the bike. I can see them sitting there sticking up out of the water. I shout out, "Conrad, what about your books?" and before I realize what I'm doing, I'm down in the river up to my waist, my legs sinking deep into the muddy bottom. I push out toward the bike. My feet slip off a slimy rock underneath and I fall forward up to my chin, but I know this old river. I swim in it every chance I get.

Even though it's not over my head here, I glide forward kicking my feet out behind me, and I reach the bike and I pull those books off and I hold them high above my head. Then I wade back to the edge of the river, slipping in the mud, falling forward sometimes. And soon enough I'm climbing back up on the shore. I've got mud up to my knees like a pair of long brown stockings and I'm all wet and there's mud on my face. I fall down on the shore among the reeds next to Conrad with the books wet but mostly safe in my arms.

I sit there next to him like something dragged from the bottom of the river. We both stay there looking at nothing at all for going on twenty minutes, and the whole time neither one of us says a single word.

It's evening now and I'm walking home along the road alone. I'm thinking about Conrad just six months ago at the beginning of the year at the height of his popularity. It was the day that our sixth-grade soccer team beat the Culpepper Coyotes, who came over in a yellow school bus thinking they were the champs. Conrad had made the winning goal that game and the next day he showed up at school with a pile of T-shirts his mama made, one for everyone in the class. (His mama makes T-shirts and sells them.) I can just see Conrad Parker Smith standing there handing out those T-shirts looking so calm and nice and sure. The T-shirts said, *Best Things in Life Aren't Things*. Didn't have anything to do with our sixth grade winning, but everybody was so happy to get a T-shirt from Conrad. They were just inside-out with joy.

I think it was Quentin Duster, the most unpopular show-off squirt in the class, who took a big Magic Marker and crossed out *Aren't Things* and put in *Is Winning*. So his T-shirt said, *Best Things in Life Is Winning*. It was a glorious triumphant time for Conrad Parker Smith. He had scored three beautiful goals, the Culpepper Coyotes had gone home with their tails between their legs, and everyone in the class was wearing one of his mama's T-shirts.

On the road here as I walk along, there's a wide field of blowing grass and there's a silver-colored weather-beaten old house sitting across from the field. On the way home, if I have time, I always go up on the porch of that house and I sit there and think, looking at the overgrown yard full of purple phlox gone wild and what Mama calls old-fashioned lilac bushes. It's a sorrowful old house and it gives me a feeling of sadness and at the same time a shiver of joy. That in my opinion is the magic combination for a poem. I write a lot of my poems on this run-down forgotten porch. I like to look in the windows into the empty quiet rooms. I always wonder who lived here and why they disappeared like the southern wind racing across these fields.

Now even though it's dusk I go up on the porch and let the wind sort of pour through my clothes. There is definitely a poem coming up from somewhere inside me. I'm just full to the brim with a poem. I keep seeing

Conrad the way he used to be, when he was everybody's favorite, walking into a room holding out his hands to a constant silent applause. Being so popular the way he was, stories used to circulate about him. Like on the hottest day of the summer last year I heard tell that Conrad had soaked his sneakers in cold water and then put them in the freezer for two hours. Then he got them out frozen solid and wore them. It felt real good, he had told everybody. Kept him cool for most of the afternoon. Before you knew it, half the kids here in West Taluka Falls were freezing their sneakers. That's the kind of popularity I'm talking about. Popularity that bordered on magnificent.

On this deserted porch with evening starting to roll in like dark fog, I can almost get a hold of that poem. Sometimes a poem will wait and hover under the surface, making me feel like I might split in two getting it out. I turn in circles now and I put my face up to the window and look into that plain dark living room. There's a wooden table near the window and it's always empty. I always wonder who sat there and what they were thinking.

But suddenly, like to jolt me right out of my poem thinking, I see something. There's a deck of playing cards on the table. They're all spread out and tossed around. There's even a few on the floor. Somebody's been in there. And here I thought this was *my* old lonely forgotten house.

chapter 4

When I get home it's dinnertime. Things are in somewhat of a disarray 'cause Mama's going to the PTA meeting to see Conrad's mother give a demonstration on how to make angels out of clothespins. (Conrad's mama makes and sells T-shirts and clothespin angels. Mama says it's not fair, some people have *all* the talent.) Mama always goes to the PTA meetings anyway. She doesn't need a bribe like clothespin angels. But some parents do. They don't just want to go and talk about the school budget. They want to *get* something out of it, come away with something.

We're kind of hurrying through dinner. Granddaddy had to make it. When it's his turn he usually cooks instant mashed potatoes and hamburger stew.

"Granddaddy'll take the easy route, if given the chance," says Mama, putting a bobby pin in her hair and sitting down at the table.

My sister Melinda's taking her sweet time not coming to the table, probably finishing up with filing her nails. Granddaddy's in the pantry getting in the refrigerator and pulling things out. So I sit down at the table, salt everything on my plate twice over, pepper everything to death, and then I say, "Are you gonna talk to Conrad's mama tonight?"

"Well," says Mama, picking up her fork. Then she stops and tastes the mashed potatoes and says, "Granddaddy, you added too much milk again. Melinda, come on out and get your dinner. We're gonna be late for the meeting, honey."

"I can't, Mama. My nails are still wet. Something's wrong with this nail polish. It isn't drying," calls Melinda from the bedroom.

"Oh, for goodness sakes. Jessie Lou, run upstairs and get my little mini hair dryer, will you? Don't bring the big one. She can use the half size on her fingernails."

"Want Mama's mini dryer?" I shout.

"No," says Melinda. "Somebody bring me a plate of food. Oh, never mind. Guess I'll skip dinner."

"I'll make you a nice sandwich, honey. We'll take it with us," says Mama.

"Will you be talking to Conrad's mama tonight?" I say again.

Mama looks over at me for a second like she's thinking about something entirely different, and then she says, "Oh, well, I suppose I will, if she doesn't get too busy. People just love those clothespin angels and they flock around her like flies to butter. Are you gonna have any sweet tea, Jessie Lou? Did you know you're supposed to get six to eight glasses of liquid per day?"

"That'd be about enough to float me halfway to China," I say. "Well, if you do talk to her, I was hoping you could ask her about Conrad's leg."

"And you too, Granddaddy," says Mama. "They say half the seniors in America suffer from mild confusion due to lack of fluids."

"Mama," I say, "I was also wondering who used to live in that old abandoned house up the road?"

"Now I haven't a clue who lived there," says Mama. "If I had an answer for every question that comes *tralala*-ing out of your mouth, Jessie Lou, I wouldn't be here, I'd be up at Buckingham Palace eating roast duck. Wouldn't I, Granddaddy?"

"I don't know," says Granddaddy. "I haven't drunk enough fluids today to be able to follow what you're talking about."

"Oh, of all the fathers to have in the world, Granddaddy, you take the prize. Doesn't he just take the prize?" says Mama, giving Granddaddy a smile.

Granddaddy gets up from the table, goes over to the counter, comes back and drops a big tub of margarine next to the pitcher of sweet tea. "I've been eating margarine instead of butter for most of my eighty-two years, Jessie Lou, and I'm not gonna stop now 'cause some old geezer at your mother's church group said it was bad for you. I heard air was bad for you too."

"Do you know anything about Conrad's leg brace, Mama? I mean whether it's permanent or not," I say.

"Now there's another one, Jessie Lou. Oh, did I fill out that form for Melinda? I swear I'm losing my mind. You know Melinda's trying out for the Junior Teen Beauty Pageant up at the Apple Blossom State Fair this year. She's gonna take the prize," says Mama, looking all proud. "Can't imagine anybody'd make a prettier picture than she does. Don't you think so, Granddaddy?"

"Beauty just shines out of that little girl's eyes," says Granddaddy.

"Anyway, I'm taking the girls over to the shopping mall in Charlottesville tomorrow so we can pick out a dress for Melinda's contest," says Mama. "See what I told you, Granddaddy? If that shopping mall at the edge of town was already built, we wouldn't even have to go that far."

"I don't see what's wrong with shopping at Muncet's down on Main Street," says Granddaddy.

"They don't have the selection," said Mama. "All they have is work boots and work shirts for the farmers. They don't have pretty little dresses for a state fair winner."

Then my older sister, Melinda, comes out of the back bedroom smelling like nail polish something awful.

"Oh, Melinda, you're trying red nail polish?" says Mama. "You're supposed to wear pink, honey. Didn't I take you over and get you color-coded? You're supposed to wear summer colors like pink. Isn't she pretty, Granddaddy?"

"She's like a little angel," says Granddaddy. "Come over here and give your granddaddy a big hug." My beautiful perfect older sister, Melinda, goes over and gives my granddaddy a hug, even sits on his old lap for a minute. "She's my little angel girl, not like you, Jessie Lou, all shorn like a puppy, all cropped off. Jessie Lou's cute though, isn't she? Cute anyway," says Granddaddy, "even with her hair all chopped off funny."

"I guess I'm just the bare old clothespin and Melinda's the angel," I say, starting to make headway on Granddaddy's hamburger stew. My granddaddy's just an old turncoat, kissing and hugging Melinda when I'm the one who takes the time to drive over to the shopping mall site every day with him. I'm the one who takes the time to check out every little change that happens over there. My granddaddy doesn't stay loyal to me even though he knows I love him so. After all, who went and bought him that sweet-smelling after-shave lotion last week when it wasn't even his birthday?

When Mama and Melinda leave for the PTA meeting, Granddaddy'll go and pretend to wash dishes but he won't get very far. He'll end up going to his room and playing the radio too loud, leaving the dishes every which way in the sink. Then I'll go up to my room and get out my journal and write me a poem about feeling like a stupid old ugly beanpole, about never being able to be perfect and pretty like my snooty older sister, Melinda.

chapter 5

First thing this morning Quentin Duster, that little scrap of a fourth grader, comes over to my table at school and holds up his newest Lewis and Clark drawing. The drawing is so big and wide it covers up most of Quentin except for his little head and those big old glasses. He's smiling away as he looks over the top of the paper at me. Then his eyes roll over to Conrad sitting on the other side of the room. Then he looks back at me and he says, "Think this drawing should receive the Cabanash County blue-ribbon art award?"

"Oh, Quentin Duster, I think you deserve the Nobel Prize," I say, crossing my arms and looking up at the ceiling. The drawing is so big I couldn't keep from looking at it even if I tried. It shows an extra-fat overstuffed dinosaur licking his lips with Clark riding on its back.

Clark is saying, "I wonder what happened to Lewis and Sacagawea?"

Quentin keeps hovering around me and then looking over at Conrad, who's sitting on the other side of the room with his back to us. Conrad's sitting *near* the popular table but not *at* the popular table. He reminds me of a rock that fell off a nice old rock wall and now that old rock is lying near the wall but it isn't part of the wall anymore. It's just a poor old rock lying in the grass.

Quentin keeps looking over at Conrad like he's got some kind of plan or something up his sleeve. It wouldn't surprise me at all if Quentin were to align himself with Conrad now in hopes of pulling himself up by his bootstraps from the deep murky lower depths of fourth grade. He knows how the winds change around here. He's seen that river. He knows a kid riding low one day could be riding high the next.

He goes off with his big drawing, avoiding our teacher, keeping his picture turned away from her. He walks past Elizabeth Parnell and Sarah Jane Peabody and Tiffany R. (not to be confused with Tiffany B., who's sitting up at the popular table). Those three used-to-be friends of mine are sitting together even tighter and closer than before. Last night their fairy tea party and special school-night sleepover got ruined by mosquitoes. An enormous swarm came in off the Cabanash River and tore into Elizabeth Parnell something terrible. She always says mosquitoes love her to death. And then Sarah Jane got a stomachache and had to lie down most of the evening 'cause they ordered pizza and it had anchovies on it by mistake. And then Elizabeth's mama set up the fairy garden tent in the living room instead of the backyard and one of the little poles broke and the tent collapsed on them in the night. Because of all that, the three of them are huddled up even closer. Mama always says tragedy brings people together, and I guess they're the living proof.

Right now our teacher writes on the chalkboard *A NEW WORLD* and she underlines it with her usual swirling line that looks like a big *Z* from one of Granddaddy's old movies, like Z for "Zorro was here."

"A new world — that's what Lewis and Clark discovered, and Sacagawea and the other Indians helped them along the way. And what were some of the things they found in the New World?" says our teacher, holding her hands together and stretching them out toward us like she's offering us an invisible bouquet of flowers. "What sort of things did they find?"

"Dinosaurs," says Quentin Duster loud and clear and smiling, looking around at the room. Everybody laughs. They just roar, and Quentin Duster settles back in his chair enjoying his great moment.

Moon n' Stars Montgomery raises her hand and says, "Lewis and Clark discovered lakes and streams and rivers and mountains."

"Ah," says our teacher, smiling, "what a miracle it must have been. Just think of it! We're going to do a little skit, a little reenactment play now."

Nathan Jones is waving his hand around and I know he wants to tell the class how his father does Revolutionary War reenactments. His father dresses up like a Revolutionary soldier and then goes into battle with a bunch of other dressed-up soldiers and Nathan sits on the sidelines wishing he could play too.

"We're going to do a little Lewis-and-Clark skit," says our teacher. She seems not to see Nathan's hand waving like a losing flag in the wind. Maybe it's because we already know about his father's reenactments. We've only heard the story six times.

"Now we need to select the cast, Lewis and Clark and Sacagawea. By the way," says our teacher, taking off her reading glasses and looking faraway out the window, "did you know that the whole time Sacagawea was leading those men through the wilderness she was carrying her young baby on her back? Yes, she had a papoose on her back. Oh, my goodness, just to think of it!"

Then she looks sad for a half a second. Mama says this year Mrs. Duster lost her husband to a skinnier woman. It came out of the blue, says Mama, and completely took her by surprise. "Okay," our teacher goes on, "write your names on a piece of paper and hand them up here and we'll put them in a hat. Somebody have a hat they can pass up?"

Ryan Ferguson, who always wears his hat with the bill pointed backward, passes up his green-and-yellow cap that says *John Deere Tractors* on it.

"There are three parts here, so cross your fingers," says the teacher, mixing the names around.

Lord love us, as my mama says, *please don't pick me*, I am thinking. If there's anything I do not want to do, it's to stand up there in front of Conrad Parker Smith stumbling over a bunch of stupid lines. It was bad enough that I couldn't say two words to him yesterday and that I threw myself in the muddy river and came up looking like something headed for the town dump and transfer station.

The teacher puts her hand in the John Deere tractor hat and pulls out a name. First she looks at it and smiles an "of course" kind of smile, and then she says, "Lewis will be played by none other than Conrad Parker Smith!" and then she expects to hear a great rousing cheer roll across the class like a ripple of wind across undiscovered America. But the room is rather quiet, almost disinterested. The popular table seems disconnected. He isn't one of them anymore. He's gotten separated off like a little old lonely boat on a big lake. One of the fourth graders, a shrimp with braids and a squeaky voice who doesn't keep up with what's going on, shouts out, "Yeah, Conrad! Way to go!"

Conrad gets up smiling, like he expected to win, like it's his natural-born right and like it would never be possible for somebody else to take the part. He turns his head toward the class in a beaming loving kind of way. He walks up there pulling that old leg brace and immediately without saying a word he becomes the great discoverer Lewis, looking out at us like we're lakes and rivers and streams, like he's not afraid of anything, like he's longing, itching, begging to discover the river to the Pacific Ocean on the other side of the continent, to hear the waves crashing and to know that there are other unknown lands beyond that.

Seeing Conrad up there, I'm just about cringing inside at the way I acted yesterday. Wish I hadn't jumped in the mud, and I'm hoping my teacher will not expect me to help Conrad with anything more. Now that his bike's gone that should be the end of it. Please let it be the end of it.

Then Mrs. Duster squeezes her eyes real tight and gives Conrad a special valentine smile and says, "Almost forgot to tell you, your mama called a little while ago and she's coming in to pick you up today." Conrad nods at her and goes on back to being Lewis.

I'm sitting here quiet as a laptop zipped up in its case, hoping I won't get picked, thinking I just got saved.

Somebody calls out, "Please, Mrs. Duster, can I be Sacagawea?"

"Wait a minute," says our teacher, pulling out another piece of paper from the hat. She looks down at it and smiles as if she's opening an Academy Award envelope for Best Actress. "The Indian girl guide will be played by Moon n' Stars Montgomery!" Sarah Jane and Louise and Elizabeth Parnell go completely insane hugging each other and jumping up and down. I guess Moon n' Stars is part of their group now that she brought in her older sister's iPod.

"Moon n' Stars! Y'all are the best!" the little fourth grader with the squeaky voice calls out. And Moon n' Stars Montgomery goes up there, pushing back her just-washed pale yellow hair, and stands next to Conrad Parker Smith. He smiles at her real kindly and he gives her a high five and I just about die. I just smolder back here at my table like a bunch of wet leaves on a campfire.

Next thing you know Quentin Duster's got the part of Clark and he's strutting up there, the shortest pip-squeak explorer you ever saw. And as soon as he stands next to Conrad, I know it's a done deal. For the last few months there's been an opening, a space, a vacancy next to Conrad Parker Smith, and for the betterment of his personal status Quentin Duster is going to try to fill that vacancy. He's gonna try to play Clark to Conrad's

Lewis, starting from now till who knows when, right here at Cabanash County Elementary.

As the afternoon wears on, I lean back and relax in my seat. Now that I know Conrad's mama is coming in today, I take a big breath that feels at first like pure sweet relief, until it gets all through me and then it changes into something almost like disappointment.

chapter 6

Granddaddy decides at the last minute to go along with us on our shopping trip to Charlottesville to get Melinda her dress for the contest 'cause he says there is a hobby shop downtown there that he wants to go in. They sell a lot of puzzles in that shop and Granddaddy loves puzzles. He's doing one of every president of the United States. He makes the announcement getting in the van that he isn't going near that shopping mall and that he wants to be dropped off outside the hobby shop and then be picked up on the way back.

"Aye-aye, Captain Ferguson," says Mama, throwing her purse in on the seat ahead of her. "Any other orders from above?"

Melinda and I are sitting in the backseat. Granddaddy shuts his door and Mama starts the engine, backing slowly out of the driveway. I know I have to get some kind of clothes to attend the contest, just to sit in the bleachers being the sister of the winner. I've kind of settled on the idea of wearing black or dark so I won't show up at all.

Halfway out of town Melinda looks over at me and says, "I have to read something at the state fair, a short thing that I wrote, like a poem or something, at the event before the judging so they can hear the sound of my voice. Mama tells me my voice is one of my strongest features."

I am sort of listening and I am kind of looking out the window at the same time at the gas stations and restaurants and antique junk shops along the way, all of them with big signs hanging on the outside saying stuff like GET IN HERE AND BUY THIS JUNK.

"Maybe by then your hair will be longer and I won't be so embarrassed to admit you're my sister," Melinda says.

"Maybe I'll cut it again," I say. "How do you know?"

"I actually have a question for you," she says and then she starts to whisper and I figure there's going

to be a punch line at the end of her question, something like "and that's why I hate you." Granddaddy and
Mama up in the front seat are listening to the radio.
The news is on. The announcer is talking about the
Iraq War and a soldier from Virginia who died this
week trying to save a bunch of other soldiers who also
died. "I was wondering," says Melinda, "if I could borrow
one of your poems, Jessie Lou? I don't write poetry. I
was wondering if I could read one of your poems and say
it was mine just for the night?"

I'm kind of taken aback by her question. I can't quite
make sense of her words. Am I missing something?
That girl hardly says beans to me and here she wants
to read one of my poems aloud at the state fair. I didn't
even know she knew about my stupid old poems. I just
write them when I need to talk but can't quite figure
out how. Don't have regular words to say, only poem
kind of words.

"'Course you can borrow one of my poems, Melinda,"
I say. "You can borrow the whole lot of them. I didn't
know anybody had any interest in them." Melinda
smiles at me for half a second and then we both go
on looking out our separate windows. On my side I am

seeing rolling green hills now and all those white zig-zagging fences and fields of running horses with their manes fanned out, rippling like silk scarves in the wind.

I was kind of stunned out of my thoughts for a second, but now I go on back to thinking about Conrad and his leg brace and how my teacher didn't say a word to me at school today about assisting him with anything. Maybe she'll forget about it entirely and let the matter just slip away. I guess I'd be pretty glad of that.

We're just passing the area outside of town where every year they hold the Cabanash County Sausage Festival and I can see they are setting up the usual German village for tomorrow, with booths and benches and little fake bridges and houses that look like Swiss chalets. One of the Bailey brothers is out on his blue tractor pulling a sausage hut on a flatbed trailer. He drives it up to the edge of the road, waves to say he wants to cross with his tractor, and Mama has to stop the van with a line of cars behind us and let him cross.

"May the wonders never cease — Frank Bailey on another one of his toys," says Mama. "Glad he isn't on that other contraption he drives. An eighty-two-year-old man on a moped makes my hair stand on end."

"Well, sugar pie, you can put your hair in curlers 'cause he's only eighty-one," says Granddaddy.

"Whatever," says Mama, putting her foot on the gas and moving on. "Rotary Club does a real nice job though. Don't you think?"

"Well, it's a lot of fun," says Granddaddy, nodding to Frank Bailey.

"Don't get any ideas, Granddaddy. I don't want you going up there horsing around this year. Last year you were up there all afternoon. You kept going back to the free sausage booth till Jean Duster had to lie and say they were sold out."

"Now what's worse?" says Granddaddy. "Eating an extra sausage or two or telling a real live lie?"

I put my head back against the seat and I open my window. The wind feels nice on my face. I guess I'd be more than thrilled never to hear my teacher mentioning me helping Conrad again.

"Jessie Lou, would you kindly close that window? You are wrecking my hair," says Melinda.

On the other hand, I'd be wicked fried zucchini with hot chili peppers if my teacher gave the job to Moon n' Stars Montgomery.

When we get to Charlottesville we leave Granddaddy off at the hobby shop to poke through all the puzzle possibilities and we drive on down through the town, which is full of college students and professors hurrying along on the sidewalk. Now Mama is heading right out of there toward the shopping mall that sits in the middle of an ocean of cars and has a big cement arched doorway in the front that reminds Granddaddy of an opening to a giant tomb.

"I suppose Granddaddy'll go up to the drugstore on the corner and buy a bunch of lottery tickets, wasting what little money he has," says Mama. "I know he gets on the phone when I'm not home and places bets on the horses, Jessie Lou. Go ahead and cover for him if you want to. I know what he's up to. I don't see the sense in it. He hasn't won but once, and then what did he do with it? Went out and bought himself a big old lawn mower he's too old to use. Where do you want to go first, Melinda, to JCPenney?"

"I don't want to buy anything, Mama," I say. "Should have left me off with Granddaddy. I could have helped him pick out a president."

"You know your granddaddy never lets anybody help him pick out anything. Besides, Jessie Lou, you *have* to get something to wear, 'cause if Melinda ends up being Miss Junior Teen at the spring state fair, they're gonna be taking pictures of the whole family."

"You'll have to wear a hat, Jessie Lou," says Melinda, making her eyes look slit-like, like a cat thinking things over.

"That's a good idea," says Mama. "You know those nice big picture hats they're making now. They say you're supposed to wear one all the time to protect your eyes from direct sunlight. 'Course they say all kinds of things."

We pull up into the parking lot at the Shenandoah Valley Shopping Mall. I always forget how many cars there are in the world. Must be millions. Once when Granddaddy was taking me to this shopping mall to get colored pencils and an art pad, we came out to the parking lot and there were so many cars we couldn't find Granddaddy's big old Chrysler Imperial. We had to get a policeman to help us.

"I'll just get something black," I say, "so I won't show up much."

"You can't wear something black in the spring," says Melinda, pulling away toward her window, making a face, and then shaking her head back and forth as if to shake that awful idea right out of her mind.

In a way I am kind of looking forward to the state fair 'cause there's a guy that does hypnotism there. He gets people to come up onstage and quack like ducks and cry like babies. Granddaddy says it's a fake. He thinks the worst of everything, but I'd still crawl on my knees all the way to Newport News if my granddaddy asked me to.

Finally we get out of the van and walk across the desert of asphalt. Heat and parking lot wind comes up around us. Mama puts her arm over each of us, one on either side. Melinda looks down at my jeans and my old sneakers and I know what she's thinking, so I just look away 'cause I don't care. I don't care at all.

chapter 7

At school our teacher writes the word DISCOVERY on the chalkboard and then she draws an arrow that points to the words SELF-DISCOVERY. "A different kind of exploration," she says, swallowing and looking happy at the same time, "an exploration into the wilderness of yourself." She whispers those last three words so they almost seem to tremble with importance.

Out the window a big truck drives by with the words CAMDEN, VIRGINIA, HOME OF THE VICIOUS VIPER VIRGINIA SAUSAGE. My mouth just about waters thinking about those tender sausages. Everybody in the class follows the truck with their eyes.

Mrs. Duster writes out the word SELF-PORTRAIT and then underlines it with another swirling Z. "What can you discover about yourself?" she says, turning around quickly from the chalkboard and looking at us real hard. We all look back at her with big wide-open eyes.

To make our self-portraits you have to lie down on a big piece of paper and somebody takes a crayon or a pencil and draws a nice outline around your whole body. Then it's up to you to draw in the details. If you feel like it, around the outside you can write words that describe who you are — like *talkative* or *funny* or *class clown*. That's what Quentin Duster writes on his margins — *TALKATIVE. FUNNY. CLASS CLOWN.* I don't see him that way. I think I would have written on his, *PIP-SQUEAKY, BOSSY, TOO BIG FOR HIS BRITCHES*. But the portraits are supposed to be what you think of yourself, not what others think of you.

After the outline around my body is finished, I pretty much hate to start putting in the details on my self-portrait. Stupid skinny-looking thing with a hedgehog hairdo. I start coloring in my worn-out blue jeans and my broken-down high-top Converse sneakers. I can never imagine myself wearing party shoes or a pretty dress like my big sister, Melinda, wears. Around the

outside in the margins I write *STUPID. UGLY. SKINNY.*
I do that partly because Ryan Ferguson is laughing and
I start hamming it up for him, forgetting for a minute that these self-portraits are going to be hanging in
the halls for our big sixth-grade graduation dance and
celebration coming up at the end of the year.

Elizabeth Parnell and Louise L., my not-right-now-
maybe-later friends, walk by and give my self-portrait
a little sneer, which means they hate it and me today,
which doesn't bother me at all 'cause I know tomorrow
they'll be just the opposite.

My pencil breaks and I have to go over to the pencil
sharpener, which is near Conrad's table. I know it seems
funny but I can barely look at him, never mind talk
to him. I halfway turn my eyes toward him and then I
look down at Conrad's self-portrait lying on the floor.
He's working away with a smooth, even look on his face.
I notice he hasn't even drawn in his leg brace. He simply left it out and around the outside he has written
POPULAR. SMART. HANDSOME.

I can tell another sausage truck just went through. I
can tell by the way the kids near the window stand up

and start staring. I guess West Taluka Falls, Virginia, wouldn't be West Taluka Falls, Virginia, without the sausage festival. You end up seeing most everybody in town there. Me, I just think it's nice to do the same thing every year and to see the same people every year doing the same thing.

Grown-ups dress up as German or Swiss yodelers with sausages to sell. All the people working there wear these special green hats. It's fun to see people from our town in a different setting, like the pale skinny man who works at the post office. He's always at the festival wearing his green felt German hat and handing out mugs of root beer. At the post office he's the guy behind the stamp window. Mama always says, "That skinny little man at the post office, Ed Collar, flirts with every single person in a skirt that comes through the door at the post office. And I pity that poor woman who works next window over from him. She has to listen to it all day. I pity her. No, I really do."

My old kindergarten teacher is always up at the festival too, handing out ice cream. (She isn't a kindergarten teacher anymore. Now she's a poodle trainer up in

Roanoke.) And I always see Mrs. Duster, our teacher, dancing her feet off in the square dance area.

Last year I went up there with Elizabeth Parnell. We were having a pretty good time kind of rambling around like we do when she happened to spot Sarah Jane Peabody on the other side of the field. All of a sudden she said she wanted to get a Super Deluxe Vicious Viper Virginia Sandwich, which is one of the hottest sausages at the festival, and she went into the Vicious Viper Sausage hut. I sat out on a bench waiting for her but she never came back out of that sausage hut. I think I waited close to an hour. When I went to look for her she had totally vanished, I mean, completely disappeared.

"There are discoveries to be made within and without," says our teacher, drawing a circle in chalk on the board. She points to the inside of the circle and then she points to the outside. Today I notice our teacher is wearing a dress with tall pine trees and lakes printed all over the fabric. I guess she's wearing that so if a little fourth grader goes up to give her a hug, that kid will be hugging the forests and rivers of Lewis and Clark.

Another sausage truck goes by out the window and everybody in the room lifts up off their seats about five inches.

"All right, yes, I know it's Friday and the Cabanash County Sausage Festival is going on this afternoon and I want you all to go there and have a good time. But I want you to go up there as explorers and discoverers like Lewis and Clark. Okay?" says our teacher.

Things start to break down. Everybody is talking at once. Teachers in the hall are shouting. Bells are ringing. Parents are peeking in from doorways. Principal is running around waving his arms. Backpacks are flying this way and that. School is over for the day.

"Jessie Lou," our teacher calls out loud and clear. I swear her quiet-loud voice could carry across canyons and valleys. "You are still responsible for helping Conrad Smith. Okay? And about that bicycle. Did it get home the way it was supposed to?"

"What?" I say.

"Did you get Conrad's bicycle home all right?"

Conrad looks over at me and I look back at Conrad and for a split-second our eyes lock tight. Tight. Then there's a moment that seems like forever, a moment of deep space when the room spins and voices chatter and I can feel Conrad's eyes on me, waiting. Waiting.

The room then seems to go silent. I look back up at Mrs. Duster and I say, "Yes, ma'am. That bike got home safe and sound."

chapter 8

Outside where the buses are loading, Quentin Duster is knocking around talking to this kid and talking to that kid, trying to get a laugh wherever he can. He sees Conrad moving across the schoolyard and he looks over at me too, coming along not exactly next to Conrad, but let's say not far off. Then Quentin Duster does what he does best. He makes a beeline right over here, kind of buzzes up alongside of Conrad, and says, "Hey, Conrad, where y'all going? Up to the sausage festival?"

"Maybe," says Conrad.

Quentin doesn't let that drop. He keeps zigzagging around me and Conrad and the more he zigzags around us, the more I realize we're moving away from the buses. Conrad isn't planning to get on that bus at all. He's planning to walk. Maybe he wants to check on his bicycle to see if it has sunk like an old refrigerator to the bottom of the river by now.

Oh, but I wish we were boarding that big yellow zoo on wheels. I know I'd feel better with those kids screaming and yelling and jumping up and down all around me. I wouldn't even care if somebody hit me on the head with a purple-striped Frisbee from the back of the bus like what happened last Friday. Anything would be better than this. I just hate walking along carrying somebody's books feeling like a stupid robot that was never programmed for speech.

Quentin keeps zigzagging and zigzagging till we're halfway down the road watching those loaded buses go by with kids making all kinds of faces at us out the back window.

"Hey, Conrad, I heard they got one of the hottest sausages the world has ever seen up at the festival this year," says Quentin. "I heard a kid fainted earlier today and had to be taken to the emergency room 'cause that sausage was so hot."

"Is that so," says Conrad, leaning down and picking up a rock off the road and throwing it fastball pitching style at a telephone pole in the distance. It looks like it's gonna hit the pole but just at the last minute it veers off and falls in the grass.

"Oh, come on, Conrad. Anybody can throw better than that," says Quentin Duster, picking up a rock and leaning back and throwing it toward the telephone pole. But it doesn't go anywhere near that pole and it doesn't land anywhere near anything at all. It's just a rock that got thrown away into the emptiness of nowhere.

"You qualify for the semifinals with that one, Quentin," says Conrad.

No matter what the situation, I can never resist throwing a rock. I've thrown going on a thousand rocks in my lifetime. Sometimes it helps me think or helps me write a poem or helps me breathe when I'm steaming up with anger. I just can't resist. Suddenly I reach down and pick up a stone and I aim at the telephone pole and I throw that rock clean and high and wide, and bingo. Bull's-eye. You can hear that rock as it smacks the telephone pole dead center. The sound ricochets through the woods.

Conrad and Quentin look at each other. Their eyes go all wide and disbelieving.

"Wow!" says Quentin Duster.

"What's that supposed to mean?" I say.

"Just means wow," says Quentin Duster. "You don't need *Webster's Unabridged Dictionary* to figure that out. Wow just means wow." Then he looks at me kind of close like he's seeing a speck of dust on my forehead and says, "What'd you go and cut off all your hair like that for?"

And I say, "Quentin Duster, go back to fourth grade and wake me up when you're gone."

"Yeah, Quentin," says Conrad, "now that you mention it, I think it *was* you I saw out on the playground yesterday chasing a little old third-grade girl with yellow curls. You had that sweet pea running around in circles."

"I didn't chase any third grader," says Quentin, putting his hands on his hips. "I don't talk to third graders."

Conrad smiles at me and I smile back.

"It's true, Quentin, I saw you too," I say.

"Well, I'm so glad y'all were focused on me yesterday," says Quentin. "And here I had no idea I was the center of your thoughts. Had I known I would have pulled up a chair and asked y'all to sit down."

"Now that would have been real polite," says Conrad, throwing another rock. It sails up high and then drops into the green murky slow lazy river with a plunk.

"Wait just a minute," says Quentin Duster, standing up on the bank of the river. "What the heck am I seeing out there, Conrad?"

Conrad looks at me and I look back and I say, "It's a bicycle, Quentin."

"Yeah," says Conrad, "don't you know that word or haven't you covered that material yet in fourth grade? A is for apple. B is for bicycle."

"No," says Quentin, "back in first grade, it was A is for apple, B is for bullroar. What's that bike doing out there in the water?"

Nobody exactly answers him. So Quentin keeps at it. "Come on, Conrad, never seen anything like it." He starts running and jumping up on rocks along the bank and then leaping down to the shore, all the time never letting up about the bicycle. "Is that the one the teacher was talking about, Conrad? What happened? Did you make a wrong turn or something?" He leaps off the rocks trying to do some sort of made-up karate maneuver and then falls into the grass along the shore.

His backpack drops down ahead of him and pops open. All kinds of junk falls out. Drawings of dinosaurs. Dinosaur cards. A pair of brand-new white Nike crosstrainers.

"Hey, where did you get the fancy shoes?" says Conrad. "Last time I saw a pair of those, they were on TV in the Division One Playoffs."

"My daddy got 'em for me up at the mall in Roanoke. Cost one hundred dollars. First time I ever had a pair of good shoes. Took me three weeks of carrying on like crazy to get 'em," says Quentin.

"Whatever," says Conrad. "They're done for now, Quentin, all covered with mud."

Quentin rolls over and gets to his feet. He looks down at the muddy shoes lying next to the river. Suddenly his face breaks up like a pie somebody just dropped on the floor. There's a fine line between a fourth grader and a baby and Quentin Duster just crossed that line. Looks like he's all prepared to throw a pre-kindergarten fit.

"Oh, gimme those things," I say, grabbing the shoes, going into my backpack, and getting out my plaid flannel shirt. I go over to the river's edge and I crouch down and let that shirt loose in the water. It swirls around waving its arms in the current and then I pull it up and wring it out nice and tight. I take that wet shirt and I scrub Quentin Duster's big white $100 shoes and soon enough the fresh mud lifts off them and those shoes look pretty new again. All the while Conrad stands there watching me looking like he needs an eye exam or something.

"There, Quentin," I say, handing him his shoes. "Quit jumping around now like a Ping-Pong ball, will you?" Quentin looks up at me for a frozen second. He takes the shoes and then he starts bolting around again like nothing happened.

Conrad doesn't say anything, picks up a rock, and skips it across the river. It hits the water seven times. Then he says, "By the way, Quentin, I heard that sausage was so hot that kid had to be airlifted by chopper all the way to Alaska, where he was put on ice for twenty-four hours."

"I heard it was Los Angeles and he had to be put in a tank of subzero water and there were sharks left in there by mistake. That's what I heard," says Quentin, smiling all over the place.

"Could be," says Conrad, looking at me and Quentin. "So are we going up there to see if we can take the heat or not?"

"You bet," says Quentin, making a running leap from one rock to another.

I feel a little like I swallowed a mouth full of blueberries too quick. Am I going with them to the sausage festival? Is that what I'm doing? If I were a being flying above us in the clouds and I looked down and saw me standing along the river with Conrad Parker Smith talking about going to the sausage festival, I'm sure that I would fall out of the sky in disbelief. I would say to myself "No way. No way. It just can't be." And then I would have to explain to myself that the only reason I'm here at all is because of that blessed beautiful metal leg brace.

Before I get back up on the road, I kind of drop my muddy wet shirt in the weeds. My mama has close to a nervous breakdown every time she finds a muddy old wet piece of clothing in my backpack, so I always think it's simpler to just throw the thing away.

Then we just start walking like we don't even know where we're going, even though we do. Somebody starts kicking a rock along the road. Somebody else makes a dumb joke, and I look up at the sky and notice suddenly what a deep blue it is.

chapter 9

"Come on, hurry up, you two. Mosquitoes are having a sit-down dinner on my back," Quentin shouts. He's pulled ahead of us on the road, rushing past the turnoff to his double-wide 'cause there's no way he wants anyone thinking he's going home. His road is called Bull's Lane, which you have to pity Quentin for, since a name like that can only lead to thousands of jokes at his expense.

"What's your hurry, Quentin? Got a flight to Washington to catch?" calls Conrad.

Quentin stops on the path, scrunches up his nose, and says, "Hey, Conrad, I heard your mama went up to the PTA meeting and showed everybody how to make those clothespin angels."

"It was just a five-minute talk to get people to come out for the meeting," says Conrad.

"Yeah, but if she gives away all her secrets, people can make their own angels and then, Conrad, you're gonna starve," says Quentin Duster.

"Not gonna starve," says Conrad.

"I guess I wouldn't even buy a stupid clothespin angel," says Quentin Duster, putting his hands on his hips, looking right up at Conrad. "What would I need such a stupid thing like that for?"

"People like 'em," says Conrad.

Soon enough we get to those fields of long blowing grass, and there sitting in its overgrown yard is that old lost-in-a-dream weather-beaten house. From a certain distance I almost feel it pulling me. I just can't look at that house but a wistful feeling blows through me. *Wistful* is my granddaddy's word. He always says to me, "Are you feeling wistful, sweetheart? Wanna talk to me? You know your granddaddy has great big ears that stick out for a reason."

We stop in the yard to rest under a big maple tree with its skirt of shade draped around it on the ground. Conrad sits down on the grass with his leg and brace kind of flung out in front of him.

After doing nothing at all in my opinion, Quentin Duster throws himself down on his back and takes a deep breath. "Ah, sure feels good to relax," he says. "Wish we were at the festival already and somebody was bringing me five sausage sandwiches laid out on a tray. We should have got a ride. Could somebody tell me what we went this way for anyway?"

"I could sure use a Vicious Viper Virginia Sausage right now," says Conrad. He puts his hand under his chin and props up his nice round face.

"Conrad," says Quentin Duster, "I don't think you could handle the Vicious Viper. For that matter, the Saucy Sally Sandwich would probably put you out of business too."

"I wouldn't know about the Saucy Sally Sandwich," says Conrad, looking sweet and sleepy, partly closing his eyes, "'cause they only sell those to third graders."

"Well, Conrad," says Quentin, "as far as grades go, I'd say you drove your bicycle like a first grader right into the river. That's what I'd say."

"Quentin, about the bicycle, let sleeping dogs lie. And if we really are going up there, we better go 'cause it closes at five," I say, and then I clear my throat because I can't believe the words came out on their own, kind of normal sounding. I clear my throat again.

"You know what I want?" says Conrad, stretching his arms up toward the sky. "I want one of those green German hats that the people that work up at the festival wear."

"Well now, you're out of luck, Conrad. That's just your tough turkey 'cause nobody gets those hats unless you work up there. People hand them down in families," says Quentin, standing up and putting his hands in his pockets. "Sorry, but that's just the way it is."

"Let's get going. We can head down through the logging trail across the field by way of a cutoff," says Conrad. "That'll take off fifteen minutes right there."

Quentin follows Conrad onto the road and I go up to the house and hop up on the porch. I pass quickly along the windows in front. I have to know if those playing cards are still in there. I kind of peer through the window into the dark front room and I see right away those cards are gone. But now there are four empty cans of soda tossed around on the old table.

*   *   *

We're just getting to the top of the hill. The sky is a freshly washed blue, cleared out by all the rains and snows and winds of winter. The redbuds are in bloom along the edge of the field, and when I look back I can still see that old house with the warm wind blowing around it.

Conrad's in the lead now, setting a slow pace because of his leg brace, and I don't mind walking even though I'm a running kind of girl. Conrad's in the lead, then me, and then hippity-hoppity four-feet-tall Quentin Duster keeping up, keeping up.

"By the way, Conrad, when you gonna get that old ugly thing taken off your leg?" says Quentin, handing us both part of a beat-up Charleston Chew candy bar.

"Can't say for sure," says Conrad. "Doctor doesn't really know. Might be going up to Charlottesville next week to see a new doctor."

"If it were me," says Quentin, "I'd just take my daddy's saw and I'd cut that old thing right off my leg and I wouldn't go to any stupid doctor."

"Not sure yet which doctor we're gonna use. Might

have to have an operation. Might even go with somebody experimental," says Conrad.

"Making you part guinea pig, Conrad," says
Quentin.

"Maybe," says Conrad.

As soon as I hear the word *doctor*, my heart starts
going like a four-wheeler, one of those fast little all-
terrain machines Granddaddy wants to buy but Mama
won't let him. Bringing a doctor into the picture is
something I didn't consider. After all, here I am getting
a chance to breathe the same old air as Conrad Parker
Smith's breathing all because of that leg brace. And I
know it's sounds awful, but I'd sort of just as soon the
leg brace stays right where it is. I pick up a rock and I
send it halfway to heaven.

Conrad pushes farther ahead of us into the brush.
He's easy to spot through the leaves 'cause he's wearing a tie-dyed pink-and-yellow T-shirt with a sunburst
pattern that says on the back *SUPPORT OUR TROOPS*.
His mama tie-dyes so many T-shirts that I've never
seen him wearing the same message twice. Some say
GET OUT OF IRAQ and others say just the opposite.

His mama wants to sell T-shirts, so she's got a selection for everybody. Conrad ends up wearing the ones that don't sell, so I don't even know which side of the war he stands on and I don't care either.

Suddenly I get all serious as we're walking along and out of nowhere I say, "My sister, Melinda, wants to read one of my poems at the state fair in the Miss Junior Teen contest and she's going to be saying it's her poem." And I fairly beam with pride, like I'm puffed up, like they say in church, "Thou shalt not be all puffed up."

Conrad says, "You *want* your older sister to read your poem and say it's her poem? You want people to think *she* wrote your poem?"

"Well, yeah," I say. "Why not? I can't be in that contest."

Quentin starts to make one of his wise-off comments about my appearance when Conrad claps his hand over Quentin's mouth. Then Quentin bites Conrad's hand and they start laughing and tumbling and rolling in the dirt, acting all stupid. I don't pay it any mind. I just stand there leaning against a tree with my arms crossed waiting for them to stop. Now they're lying on their backs laughing like a couple of hyenas.

Conrad's pink-and-yellow shirt is all covered with dirt. Conrad is the only boy on the face of the earth who can wear a pink T-shirt and carry it off. Doesn't bother him in the least. Doesn't even faze him. You know what that is? That's deep down *popular*.

chapter 10

"Are we getting closer or farther away from those sausages?" says Quentin. "I mean, Conrad, are you one of those people who can't find their way out of a paper bag or what?"

"This trail goes down through the woods and comes out right by the festival," says Conrad. "Before you know it you're gonna be up to your ears in onions and fried peppers."

Now the logging road is taking a turn over a small hill and then dips down into the lazy spring woods. Just as we're coming around a bend on the shady path, a great long-legged heron lifts up over the trees and flies toward the river. Quentin is singing off-key, "Zippity doo dah, zippity ay. My, oh my, what a wonderful day. Plenty of sunshine heading my way . . ."

Conrad says, "And first place choral award goes to . . ."

Suddenly Quentin stops. "Hold up a second," he says. "Did you hear something or is it just me?" We quiet down for a minute and stand there. Yes, we do hear something, something coming from the middle of the enclosed, tucked-away field. There are woods on all sides of that field — maples, oak, a few birches in among the redbuds.

We definitely hear *something*. It's a knocking sound. Yes, something is in the field. I look at Conrad and Quentin and they both look back at me.

"Now, what do you suppose that noise is?" says Conrad, laying his head back easy and slow.

"Fifty-four woodpeckers working on the same tree," says Quentin, throwing one of his hare-brained rocks up and away into nowhere.

"Hush, now," says Conrad, looking back at us. "You know what we're doing? We're making a discovery. Teacher's gonna be real pleased. We're just doing our homework."

Leg brace or not, Conrad's a natural-born leader.

He pushes a few branches back that have grown across the logging trail just like Lewis himself would have done.

I can't say Quentin looks much like Clark now, huffing and puffing and throwing himself around. As we get nearer, the knickety-knocking noise gets louder.

Now from the darkness of the woods we can see the sunlight in the field, and fifty yards from us in the center of the field we see something. It's big, kind of long and tall, and half wrapped up in a plastic tarp that's blowing around. It's high up on wheels, and somebody's standing there wearing a pair of greasy coveralls.

"Dibs on this for my discovery report," whispers Quentin. "I could pull an A with this one."

"Is that Tiny Bailey?" I say.

"Yes, ma'am," says Quentin. "Wears size eighteen shoes and he's a fifth-year senior up at the Vocational Center. They call him 'The Engine' up there 'cause he likes to work on stuff. My cousin knows him."

"Well, Quentin, with friends in high places like that, next thing we know you'll be hosting your own miniseries," says Conrad, putting his arm over Quentin's bony little shoulder.

"Yeah, and I'm gonna get me an A on my report. Maybe I'll even get on the honor roll and get to go up to Roanoke and eat ice cream with the smart kids," says Quentin.

"Could be," says Conrad, "miracles do happen."

"My report is going to be so great, I might be asked to give a speech for the sixth-grade graduation this year," says Quentin.

"Well, Quentin, if you're gonna talk the talk, you better walk the walk," says Conrad. "I heard you never do your homework at all."

"What do you think Tiny's doing?" I say.

Around here, not much goes on of any interest. Once in a while we see a deer. Quentin's daddy saw a bobcat in broad daylight a while back. You hear coyotes at night but you never see them. The biggest thrill we had this winter was when Granddaddy won double bingo twice in one night at the Russell Lee Senior Center and came home with a new Weber grill and five fancy picnic place mats cut in the shape of a burger on a bun.

"Maybe he's repairing an alien spacecraft that landed here by mistake," says Quentin. "It's long and skinny and it's on wheels. Could be alien."

"What's a big old guy like that got a name like Tiny for anyway?" says Conrad.

"He's the great-nephew of the Bailey brothers," says Quentin.

"'Cause he's big. That's why they call him Tiny," I say.

"How do you know?" says Conrad.

"'Cause I write poems and things come to me. My granddaddy says I've got three eyes," I say.

"Yeah, and they're all crossed every which way," says Quentin, smiling at me and crossing his eyes.

"Hush now," says Conrad, "we're making a discovery. This more or less fell in our lap. Let's move up a little closer to see better."

When Conrad makes a suggestion, it always holds water. We move forward. We sit down in the ferns and bushes and we watch Tiny working. The noisy blue tarp makes it harder to see anything, and we keep fighting over what he might be doing. We also try to take notes for our discovery report without any paper. Finally we write a few things down on the back side of the

Charleston Chew candy wrapper. Quentin continues to stand firm on his stupid space-alien theory. I don't say anything about the cards and cans of soda I saw up at the old house.

"We need to come back tomorrow with my grand-daddy's digital camera," I say.

"No, seriously, Conrad," says Quentin, "what do you really think Tiny's doing? I mean, why would a teenager like that be working down here in this out-of-the-way field, if he wasn't hiding something?"

chapter 11

By the time we get back on the path, it's getting late. We don't say anything more about Tiny Bailey. We just kind of let that simmer in a covered pot. Like Mama says when Granddaddy starts talking off-the-wall politics, "Put a lid on it, Granddaddy."

"Let's keep moving," says Conrad, rubbing his tummy and looking up at the sky. "Sausages are calling my name."

"Yeah, come to think about it," says Quentin, smiling up at Conrad, "I did hear some voices calling out *Big Idiot, Big Idiot, Big Idiot.*"

The trail turns out to be longer than Conrad remembered. We get caught in a bunch of bushes full of burs that are blocking the way and we end up yipping and yapping down in the woods like a bunch of junkyard dogs. I just skinned my knee and I know my mama will have a fit. She'll say stuff like "Jessie Lou, if you skin your knees one more time, you're always gonna have to wear dark panty hose and full-length skirts when you grow up."

Finally the trail breaks through the woods. We're right at the highway, and we can see the big green flag pumping back and forth in the wind, displaying the words CABANASH COUNTY KNOCKWURST SAUSAGE FESTIVAL.

There's an evening mist starting to form over the field, and there are strings of plastic lanterns glowing in the almost dark. Because we're so late some of the booths are closing up shop, but we get in line and we secure a sandwich each, hot and bubbly and juicy. Quentin can't wait and tears into his right away.

We sit on the side of a hill to eat our sandwiches. Accordion music is playing nearby. It's a sweet but sad sound all at the same time, and I smell the delicious smell of smoke off the sausage grills and I remember the time Mama took us camping along the Cabanash River and Granddaddy caught a big trout and we had a campfire. The smell of smoke makes me feel like this day with Conrad is already kind of a hazy memory, tangy and spicy like the sausage sandwiches, mild and sweet like the smell of smoke.

I turn around and see that old leg brace snug tight around Conrad's leg and I whisper to myself, *Thank you thank you thank you.* I try not to think about that old stupid experimental doctor up in Charlottesville. For all I know he could be a quack. He sounds like one, ready to operate on anything that comes his way.

Some of the popular kids are crossing a little fake bridge that's painted green and yellow with pictures of sausage sandwiches all along it. Those five kids seem to be bored and cool and excited all at the same time. They don't even look this way. Like maybe we're in a time warp and we're truly invisible to them. Suddenly thinking of me as "we" feels scrumptious and warm and soothing and I don't want it to go away.

The festival is shutting down. Two people walk by us carrying a big piece of plywood with a painting of a little old German cottage on the front. The whole German village is being dismantled and carried off before our eyes.

Quentin looks sick as a dog, kind of yellowish gray, and he's sitting there frowning and eyeing Conrad. I turn my head to see what he's looking at and right away I see that Conrad's wearing one of those green felt hats with the feather on the side. "Where did you get that hat, Conrad? Thought you had to be German to get your hands on one of those."

"Some guy gave it to me as he was packing up his booth," says Conrad, looking cheerful.

And I think to myself, *Isn't that the way it is.* Things just kind of come to Conrad naturally. Adults see him and they want to give him everything they've got. Like I said before, there's just something I-don't-know-what about Conrad Parker Smith.

chapter 12

Next day, what do you know? Granddaddy wins thirty-five dollars on one of the horses he bet on over the telephone. "Big deal," I can hear Mama saying as soon as I get on the porch, "that doesn't make me like gambling any more than I did before."

Granddaddy is all bright and perky, tilting his head, looking like he's ready to break into a Virginia reel or a do-si-do when I walk in the back door. "We're going to be eating dinner tonight at the Tex-Mex Restaurant on Milton Avenue courtesy of your granddaddy," says Granddaddy. "Tell your sister to get on down here and get her shoes on."

But it's Saturday and Mama and Melinda are supposed to be going to a Martha Nottingham Cake Mix party tonight, hosted by Quentin Duster's mother. It's the only way you can purchase all the Martha Nottingham products. Granddaddy thinks the Martha Nottingham instant mashed potatoes blow all other instant mashed potatoes out of the water. We use a lot of those mixes and they're better than what you get in the store. Melinda helps take the orders and she told me some people spend as much as two hundred dollars a night. Plus it's more or less a social event.

I am hoping Conrad's mother will be there and that she might finally tell my mother a little about Conrad's situation, when and if he is going to have the operation on his leg and all that. It is gnawing at me just as if it was a little mouse eating a kernel of corn inside me. I can just feel the gnawing worry. I am worried 'cause I don't want anything to go wrong, and at the same time I don't want anything to go exactly right either. Meaning that I don't want him to get all fixed up before I even have a chance to get to know him. The way I see it, Conrad could either die in some crackpot operation or he could get repaired. In either case I figure I'm holding a losing card. In terrible penance for my ugly mean thoughts, I went and cut off my bangs even shorter this morning. I hacked them crooked and then I looked in the mirror and I hated it. I just hated it.

"Fred Bailey called a little while ago," says Granddaddy, leaning on the kitchen counter. "Guess all that figuring finally paid off. My horse came in third, Jessie Lou. So I hope everybody's starving to death right now and ready to take it to the top Texas style."

"I'm so hungry, Granddaddy," I say, "my stomach feels like an empty parking lot, like you could drive a big old tractor trailer truck through it right now and I wouldn't take notice. That's how starved I am."

"Granddaddy, Melinda and I have our Martha Nottingham Cake Mix party tonight," says Mama. "We'll eat over there. You and Jessie Lou go on alone. That way you can critique the food the way you like to and I won't have to listen to all that gourmet nonsense."

Outside it is beginning to rain. I can hear it on the roof and I can see it falling in sheets of green past the window. Good thing for the rain because the daffodils in our yard are looking twisted, bending over in rows like they're praying for water.

Mama puts on her rain jacket and Granddaddy helps Melinda put on her pink vinyl raincoat with little red hearts printed on it and the repeated words stamped all over it as a design: *Love ya, Love ya, Love ya, Love ya.* Melinda puts on her little matching hat and she looks about like Barbie's little sister going out for a Sunday stroll. She has her little bookkeeping satchel with her and she completely forgets to say good-bye to me.

Mama opens the front door and the rain falls like a curtain in front of her. She holds her hand out to test the strength of it and then she walks right out into it, calling back, "Jessie Lou, you keep your granddaddy out of that hardware store. Old as they are, those Bailey brothers continue to be a bad influence."

Granddaddy and I don't pay a whole lot of attention. He looks away and I'm wishing I could call out, "Mama, talk to Conrad's mother. Find out when he's going in for his operation." But then another van pulls up along the front of the house. It is full of Martha Nottingham

Cake Mix buyers waving and calling to Mama. So I let it go. And both vans drive off honking.

Granddaddy is nodding good-bye and smiling at everybody and then, as soon as they drive off, he rubs his hands together and says, "Let's hit the road, kiddo. I've got to get over to the hardware store and pick up my winnings." Granddaddy can't wait to see his big buddies Fred and Frank Bailey, but Mama thinks they do nothing but rile Granddaddy up, talking to him about which horse is going to win and why, when according to Mama, they haven't got a clue about any of it.

It is still rainy and miserable by the time Granddaddy and I get out to his big old white Chrysler Imperial. Mama calls it "an old gas guzzler." But Granddaddy *loves* his car. It's one of those ones with the stick shift on the steering wheel. Mama won't let Granddaddy drive alone anymore. He has to have a passenger with him to keep him alert or she thinks the cops will pick him up. So he's always pestering me to drive this place and that place with him. I always say I will, but Melinda always says she's got to do her homework — can't do this and can't do that. Too busy with this and too busy with that. Too busy with nothing. That's why it burns me up when Granddaddy covers her with kisses.

We drive through the rain. Old windshield wipers working so hard to keep the blur out of the picture ahead of us. Old windshield wipers sound to me like they're saying over and over again as they flip back and forth, "What-a you gonna do? What-a you gonna do? What-a you gonna do?"

Granddaddy pulls his car up to park it downtown on Main Street and it bumps the curb and then it bumps against the car in front of us. Granddaddy looks at me and says, "Don't you tell your mama."

It's still raining terrible awful when we get out of the car. We have an old umbrella with us, but the rain is so fierce it seems to be pelting from above *and* below and it comes in under our umbrella like it's raining up from the sidewalk. The wind pulls us along, drags us down the street.

We get under the awning at Bailey's Hardware Store and we stand there a minute looking out at the town, waiting for the umbrella to lose some of its water. It's raining so hard all the colors along the street appear to be blurry gray or brown or black.

We stand there a moment looking out at the rain and staring across the street at the stores over there. I'm looking right at the window of Muncet's Clothing. Even though it's fifty percent coveralls and hunting jackets, Melinda always goes in there and comes out with some itchy-looking lavender thing. Mama says Melinda has a knack for finding pastels. "In among those work shirts, Melinda has a way of finding pretty little ecru slippers you'd never know were there," says Mama. "I call that a natural-born coordinating talent."

I'm just kind of standing here listening to the rain when suddenly I see Conrad Parker Smith and his mama coming out of a door across the street that leads to the upper floors where there are all kinds of dark mysterious offices. They're both wearing those red T-shirts of his mama's that say *Best Things in Life Aren't Things*. His mama made way too many of that one. Conrad told me they have boxes and boxes of that T-shirt and they are looking to get rid of them.

Now his mama's waiting on the corner under another awning while Conrad pulls that old leg brace along in the rain. He's moving slower than he was yesterday. His leg must already be worse. I get a terrible sorrowful feeling when I see that, but at the same time I'm crossing my fingers that wasn't a doctor's office they just came out of.

Conrad doesn't see me. Just as well. I don't think I'd know what to do if he did see me. I stand here watching them disappear down the street in the rain, and I bite the inside of my lip and I scratch off two healed-up scabs on my arm.

Granddaddy rubs his hands together and says, "Shall we go on in, Jessie Lou, or you want to stay out here and get soaked?"

"I'll go in too, Granddaddy."

As I walk in the store, I look to the back and see the long wooden counter and silver cash register and both Bailey brothers, and I can see their big old great-nephew Tiny sitting behind them in a rocking chair reading a comic book. On second thought, maybe it isn't a comic book. Looks more like a how-to book. Wish I could see from here just what he's reading up on. Today Tiny looks all drowsy and innocent just sitting there in his great-uncles' store reading away, like he isn't secretly working on anything at all down in that pretty little meadow.

I follow Granddaddy toward the back of the hardware store. It's dark and smells of oil and metal and there are walls and walls of bins full of nails and bolts and tools — tools to build birdhouses, to fix plumbing, to rake leaves. You come in here with all the plans you have in your heart and these tools will help you bring those plans to life, like the time Granddaddy built me that doll dresser. He made the plans and then he came in here and bought all the stuff and then he built the doll dresser for me and I still have it. I'll keep it till the day I die.

I don't go all the way to the back to the old cash register where Granddaddy is talking to Frank and Fred Bailey. They are talking low and fast. Granddaddy is acting all important about the various horses, coming on like an authority 'cause he won. Then Fred or Frank Bailey opens the cash register and the bell rings and he pays Granddaddy in cash.

I've been in this town my whole life and I've never been able to figure out which brother is Frank and which is Fred. They're not twins, but you can't tell them apart. Now that they are in their early eighties, they look even more alike. Mama says one of the brothers, Fred, got married out of school, settled down real nice, and stayed married, while the other brother, Frank, had a sports car, dated all kinds of women, and stays married even today just by the skin of his teeth. He's the one who has the moped. Makes Mama crazy when he drives over on it and picks up Granddaddy and they shoot off together in all that smoke and noise.

"You stay on back there, Jessie Lou. I'll be right with you. You be a good girl now," Granddaddy calls.

Well, I'm standing by a wooden tray filled with big chunks of soft blue chalk to use when you're dropping a plumb line down a wall. Granddaddy told me you mark your line off with this nice big blue soft chalk. The blue is almost the color of the cornflowers that grow along the road in August. I pick up a piece and I kind of draw a line along the wooden bin. I wonder as I stand here waiting for Granddaddy, I wonder if Big Box Home and Hardware would ever have a wooden bin full of nice old big pieces of chalk like this.

When Granddaddy and I get back from the Tex-Mex Restaurant, it's raining even harder. A deer sails right over the hood of the car and I can see its face up close, its eyes wild and frightened. But it makes it, leaps right over the big Chrysler Imperial, and disappears into the woods not far from the old abandoned house.

At home Mama and Melinda are playing cards at the kitchen table, drinking ginger ale with ice cream in it, using straws. Other times in my life I would have been miserable at such a sight, but I have other things to think about.

"Conrad's mother go tonight?" I ask soon as we get in the door, half hoping she'd been on her way over there when I saw them earlier.

"No," says Mama. "She's on one of her down cycles. Doctor wants her to go on low carbs."

"Oh," I say.

"Did you enjoy the new restaurant, Granddaddy? Jean Duster says it's excellent," says Mama, sipping her ginger ale float.

"Well, it was all right except that it wasn't a Tex-Mex place at all," says Granddaddy. "There weren't any Texans running it. They were a bunch of folks from Buchram, Virginia. I saw them back in there. They cooked up the fakest Mexican food I ever had. I thought I was eating hush puppies."

"Granddaddy," says Mama, standing up for a minute and throwing her arms around him, giving him a big kiss, "I knew you wouldn't like it. You never like any restaurants. Fact is, you don't like anything."

"That's not true," says Granddaddy. "I like you and Melinda and Jessie Lou."

"Sure would be better if you'd open up your heart to the world around you, Granddaddy," says Mama, sitting back down and looking at the cards in her hand.

Then Melinda looks at me with her prizewinning green eyes going all shady and dark. "Did you and Granddaddy have a good time?" she says.

"The best," I say, smiling.

chapter 13

Monday morning on the school bus seems like more than I can stand today. Kids are all riled up, still bragging about how many sausages they ate on Friday and what they saw on TV last night. I'm way toward the back of the bus keeping clear of the flying peanuts somebody's throwing. From where I am, I can see Conrad and Quentin sitting together up toward the front of the bus. Quentin is talking away, while Conrad's turned around trying to include everybody around him.

Brice Buttonwood is making jokes and handing out selected white envelopes having something to do with his daddy's second bowling alley in the new shopping mall and the grand opening coming up there next month. Kids like Tiffany B. just got handed a white envelope and she looks all happy and important. I can see Conrad looking around smiling, expecting the best. He waves to Brice and Brice kind of nods back, but I don't see any envelope being passed up that way.

Sitting all alone back here feels like what I'm used to, and when I look up ahead at Conrad and Quentin, they seem a million miles away, like that sausage festival was a dream, a fluke, a wild card that got tossed my way by mistake. I almost wish it was after school right now and I was just getting off the bus and going into the house smelling those quick-thaw Shake 'n Bake chicken snacks cooking, getting ready to play a hand of crazy eights with my granddaddy. But I guess he isn't gonna even be home today 'cause he's going on a senior citizens' walkathon over in Waynesboro.

All the rest of the way to school, I keep my head low, looking out the window, thinking about those discovery reports and feeling unsure 'cause I don't even know if I'll be talking to Conrad again.

When I finally get off the bus and go into my class, the teacher is just leaving the room. Everybody's kind of sitting there while she goes off to talk with the principal about something "very exciting."

As soon as there's a pause, who goes up to the blackboard but Quentin Duster himself. He starts drawing a big gooney boy's face and then a gooney-looking girl's face and under it he writes *Conrad Smith and Moon n' Stars Montgomery*. Then he writes underneath it, *TRUE LOVE*. Conrad wads up last week's math homework into a ball and throws it at Quentin's head.

Just then we hear some heavy footsteps outside the door, and we turn and see Tiny Bailey lumbering on down the hall nice and slow. Quentin's head spins around. He looks like a human question mark standing there. He drops his chalk on the floor, and our teacher comes back into the room smiling. She steps unknowingly right on the chalk and I can hear it go crunch and shatter under her foot. She keeps on smiling. She's wearing her Lewis and Clark forest and lakes dress, and the way she's leaning forward with her arms crossed in front of her and her hands lying up near her throat, it looks like there's something important inside her, like a bird that's pressing to fly out.

She says, "Today because of a mix-up in a schedule and a cancellation, we have been told that this year we will be hosting the All-State Marching Bands here in West Taluka Falls! Those of you who are taking band will be able to participate in All-State even if our band hasn't normally qualified in the past."

Mrs. Duster might be putting that mildly. There are some who say our band is the absolute worst in the state. But everybody cheers and thumps the floor with their feet. Mrs. Duster swallows and smiles and folds her hands together in front of her like they are just a pair of soft, pliable gloves.

"This is upon us very quickly," says Mrs. Duster. "We will be hosting All-State next week! We have to move fast and we have to move with precision. This is indeed an honor for us."

Almost every kid in the class is taking an instrument. This fall I told Mr. Muzzle, our band teacher, that I wanted to play the trumpet, and I'm the only girl in the trumpet section. Mama always looks a little strange when I go to practice and she usually says, "Honey, would y'all mind practicing out on the porch tonight? I have what you call an over-the-counter stress headache."

"This will mean," our teacher goes on, "even at this late notice that all students in the band will be receiving some kind of marching band outfit."

Everybody cheers again and Ryan Ferguson throws his John Deere tractor hat up to the ceiling and it falls back down and lands perfectly of all places on Quentin Duster's head. Quentin stands there with his arms out to show amazement. He turns in circles, making like everyone's cheering for him.

After school we are all supposed to go over to the library meeting room upstairs and get our music and instructions from Mr. Muzzle. Soon as the bell rings, everybody goes in the coatroom next to our class and starts grabbing trombones and flutes and French horns and taking off. I get in there and all I see are heads and hands and black instrument cases flying every which way. When the dust settles, I'm standing there looking straight at Conrad Parker Smith. He's got his saxophone case and his backpack and his jacket and a couple of extra books in his arms and right now he's reminding me of an old-fashioned loaded-down coatrack about to tip over. I grab a bunch of extra stuff from Conrad, and Quentin Duster pops up from behind a pile of coats. Then the three of us kind of fall in together, heading down the hall, dragging our old instrument cases over to the library.

Quentin Duster looks like he's gonna need a U-Haul truck to get his big tuba over there, but it turns out he's got little wheels on his case. (Quentin Duster has a way of getting around any kind of work, in my opinion.)

"Hope to take a minute to get on the computer at the library and play some Pac-Man," says Quentin. "There may be bigger and better computer games out there, but I'm the undisputed Pac-Man expert and champion."

"Yeah, Quentin," says Conrad, "I've seen you over there, playing Pac-Man for hours on end till your eyes are just two big glazed-over cookies right out of the oven."

Halfway across the soccer field, we see big old Tiny Bailey working his way toward the library too. Then Conrad and Quentin and I look right at each other like we're seeing gold stars on our discovery reports, like the gold stars are just falling from the sky and all we have to do is reach out and catch them.

"What the heck is old Tiny coming around here for?" says Conrad, lugging his leg brace and his saxophone.

"Beats me," says Quentin, "but I think it might have something to do with the fact that he plays the jumbo bass drum and Mr. Muzzle says we don't have any jumbo bass drum players this year."

"Could be," says Conrad.

"But it's not gonna help much 'cause our band still sounds like a bunch of sick dogs," I say.

"Hey, Tiny, nice day!" Quentin calls out, kind of shoving ahead of Conrad.

I nudge Quentin with my elbow and he squeals like a stuck pig, and Tiny goes into the library and shuts the door. By the time we get in there, he's gone.

We walk into the nice old library, same one my granddaddy used to use when he was young. Immediately Quentin and Conrad start giggling 'cause we're supposed to be quiet. A teenager who helps out here comes over to us and says in a real hushed tone, "You're supposed to wait over there till the trombone players come down from the upper reading room."

"Okay," I say, nudging Quentin again. There are fourteen trombone players at Cabanash County Elementary and they're all tone-deaf. With a trombone, you slide that lower piece back and forth, and in my opinion it's just pure dumb luck if you hit the right note.

We go over near the tall window, and Conrad sits down and puts his saxophone case up on the big oak table in front of him, old oak panels all around us on the walls.

Along the other end of that table is Moon n' Stars Montgomery sitting there doing her homework. Today her hair is the color of the moon in an early morning sky. I look over at Conrad and then I look at her and a cold wind blows through my heart.

Moon n' Stars gets herself all A-pluses and never misses a day of school even though she does have a hippie for a mama. Last spring on Earth Day when she came to school to pick up Moon n' Stars, her mama was wearing a big green Earth outfit, a big fat globe kind of thing, bulging out all around her. She had a sign hanging around her neck that said SAVE THE EARTH. She had a hat on her head that was supposed to represent our damaged ozone layer, but it just looked like a big dirty old hat to me.

Conrad looks over at Moon n' Stars now like the sun nodding to the moon. I look away, trying to think about something else like All-State coming up next week and how I can't wait to march along playing my trumpet as loud as I want to with the wind in my face.

Quentin says, "Wonder where Tiny went now."

Conrad says, "I don't know, Quentin. Put a discovery report on two legs and what have you got . . . nothing but trouble."

I lean over to Conrad and whisper across the table to him, "Go over and ask Miss Ferguson if she knows what kind of books Tiny's been taking out recently. Well, I saw him reading a book at his great-uncles' store, didn't I? Tiny's not the kind of guy to go out and buy a book."

Conrad raises his eyebrows at Quentin and Quentin shrugs his shoulders and looks back at him. So Conrad shoves his chair back, making a tremendous scraping sound in the quiet of the room, which Quentin decides is the funniest thing he ever heard. "I can't just go ask her that," Conrad says.

"Well, think of *something*," I whisper.

As a testament to Conrad's intelligence, he goes over to the checkout desk and looks at Miss Ferguson and says, "I heard the book Tiny Bailey was reading was real good and I wanted to read it next. Can I get on the wait list for that book?"

"Well," says Miss Ferguson, pulling out Tiny Bailey's library card, "Tiny Bailey hasn't taken a book out of the library since he was in fifth grade some eight years ago. At that time he had a book out called *Creeping Crawling Spiders* by Harrison Gillis. There isn't a wait list on it at all. Do you want me to get that book for you, Conrad?"

"Uh, maybe," says Conrad, and Quentin starts giggling and squirming and I kick Quentin under the table and he shouts out "Ouch." And then Conrad starts laughing, and Moon n' Stars looks up from her notebook, and Brice Buttonwood rolls through with his spiffy piccolo case. (All the popular kids play piccolos or flutes. I'm not exactly sure why. Maybe it's because they just naturally gravitate toward that high-pitched stuck-up sound.) Finally the fourteen trombone players come trooping through, looking kind of gloomy.

"Okay," says Miss Ferguson, "time for the next group to go up to the reading room. Just follow me."

Conrad and I follow her. Quentin hangs to the back, staying clear of Miss Ferguson, and I know why. He has a library book about dinosaurs that is two years overdue under his bed somewhere in a box. And that book is so badly overdue that Quentin freezes up when he thinks about it and won't even lean over and *look* to see if it really *is* under his bed, never mind bringing it in and paying up.

Conrad and I and then Quentin follow Miss Ferguson up the creaky old back stairs. At the top of the stairs there's a big glass cabinet full of all kinds of stuffed used-to-be-live animals looking at you like to break your heart. There's a skunk and a raccoon and a little old red squirrel sitting up, looking at you and holding a nut. My mama says all those stuffed creatures were there when she was a little girl. That same little red squirrel's been sitting up, looking at you, hoping to find a way out of that cabinet for going on fifty years.

Miss Ferguson opens the big old creaking door to the upper reading room. First thing we see is Mr. Muzzle, our band teacher. He's over by the chalkboard glaring at a group of French horn players.

There's a second grader lying on the floor reading a book, and there is a row of flute and piccolo players practicing their snooty scales. Tiny Bailey looks even bigger than usual tucked into one of the band chairs at the back of the room with his jumbo bass drum in front of him. He's tapping his foot to the beat, and I look down through the aisles at his shoes and they *are* enormous. Quentin had told me earlier, "I heard Tiny Bailey's feet are so big he has to mail away to Richmond for all his footwear."

Quentin squeezes between us and hurries in ahead to sit next to Tiny Bailey. He gives me and Conrad a big stupid-looking smile, arches his eyebrows way high, and does his usual thumbs-up.

"Okay, people," says Mr. Muzzle as soon as we get into the room and find a chair. "We're a marching band now. What does that mean? It means we're marching and we're marching in step. It means no one lags behind. It means form is everything. It means counting one, two, three, four, keeping in step with the people on either side. No messing up."

About ten minutes into the class, Conrad gets up and leaves the band room with Mr. Muzzle calling out, "One, two, three, four. Pick up your feet!"

I get up too and follow Conrad. He goes out into the hall and stands at the window and I stand next to him. From where we are, we can see the construction site at the edge of town clear as a bell and we can see Big Box Home and Hardware. It looks bigger and better than last time. It's all bright and shiny and enticing, with that gray sea of parking lot wrapped around it soft as a blanket. I can just imagine all the locals in the area flocking to it like geese to a pond. I bet my old granddaddy and the Bailey brothers would crumple up and cry if they could see how good that shopping mall looks today.

Conrad puts his face up close to the window. I know it's the marching aspect to the band that has him feeling blue. I know he knows he can't keep that pace with his leg brace. Conrad runs his fingers over his face.

"Guess I'm quitting band for now," says Conrad.

"Me too, Conrad," I say. "All-State is a bunch of bull."

chapter 14

This week started off pretty crazy 'cause Melinda and Mama went up to Newport News for two days to take Melinda to a special hair salon so they could get ideas on hairstyles for the contest. While they were up there, they went to a fashion show put on by the American Legion Auxiliary and Melinda got a free basket of bath soaps. On top of that, our teacher was out for a day and we had a substitute who kept saying to Quentin Duster, "Clifford, I do not abide by talking in class."

All this week every day Conrad and Quentin and I have been meeting up after school and we've been watching Tiny Bailey work, but except for getting a couple of blurry digital photos of him with a wrench in his hand, we haven't turned up much.

Sometimes when we're out there in the fields, I look around at the grass blowing and the clouds sailing along and I see myself sitting there next to Conrad Parker Smith and then again I have to explain to myself how this came to happen. I have to remind myself that Conrad isn't popular anymore and then I think how *glad* I am that he isn't popular anymore and how much I want him to stay unpopular. And then I feel terrible that I could have such a miserable outlook for somebody else.

Today we're walking through the field on the other side of the road from the old silvery house. "Why don't we just go up to 'The Engine' and say, 'Hi, Tiny, what are y'all doing down in that field anyway?'" says Quentin.

"'Cause he wouldn't tell us," says Conrad. "We've walked into a full-blown secret. Let's face the facts. We're probably looking at at least an A on our report if we can find out what's going on." Conrad throws another one of his light-as-a-bird high-flying rocks. I just have to admire that perfect arc.

I come up just ahead of him to match it and I throw a rock a hundred feet, my best ever, and hit another telephone pole bull's-eye. I can't believe I threw it that far. I'm jumping up and down, but when I turn around, Conrad and Quentin aren't even looking my way. I'm staring at the backs of their heads. Conrad's head is higher up, his light-colored hair feathery and soft and lying against his neck. Quentin's head is much lower down. It's a little head with sheared hair that his daddy cuts for him once a month. I'm looking at those two heads turned away and I'm saying, "You should have seen that rock I just threw, Conrad. It just about went around the moon and back."

But Conrad doesn't answer. He's staring over toward the trees. Finally he says, "Was it my imagination or did you just see Frank Bailey go down into those woods?"

"No," says Quentin, "I didn't see Frank Bailey. I saw Fred Bailey."

"Whatever," says Conrad. "One of those Bailey brothers went down there. Never seen them in these fields before."

Like I said, nothing ever happens around here. Biggest event last year was when the housekeeper for Reverend Morris put up a clothesline on the front porch of the house right on Main Street and hung out fourteen pairs of the reverend's worn-out underwear, fourteen dingy white briefs swinging in the wind. People in this town went into an uproar about it. It turned out, Mama said, that the reverend's housekeeper was bipolar and she'd forgotten to take her meds. Mama said it brought on a kind of mini nervous breakdown. Soon as she got back on her meds, she was all proper again, and so long as she stays on them, her job is secure. During that time, I heard some dumb kid told Quentin Duster bipolar had something to do with bears. That was it. That was the biggest event of last year.

I look back at Conrad and then I look over at Quentin and then Conrad makes a sign, a waving motion for us to follow him, and we do. Softly. Softly. And ever so swiftly, even with the leg brace. A small pack of antelope. Three loping silent coyotes. Yes, we follow. Oh lord, nothing could keep us away. Not anything, certainly not Mama saying, "Honey, all week I want you home tagging stuff to put in Jean Duster's yard sale."

"It was too Fred Bailey," whispers Quentin, "'cause he's a little bit skinnier than Frank."

"Frank Bailey has that bump on his nose," says Conrad, "and even from this far away, I'm sure I could see it."

"He's got to be headed down to that field. Let's take the shortcut. I'll race you down there. Betcha I get there first," says Quentin, looking at us, all revved up with his arms poised for action.

"Go ahead," says Conrad, throwing his head back and looking down at Quentin. "I'm not in any big hurry."

"Go on, Quentin," I say, "it's too hot to run. We'll see you down there in a couple of minutes." It's hard for me to give up a race 'cause I love them so, but I hold myself back for Conrad's sake, even though I know Conrad has kind of gotten used to not being first anymore. He can come in last and it doesn't matter at all to him, because in his heart he knows *first* isn't touching a doorknob or getting to sit in the front seat by the window or making it up to the road before everybody else. *First* is something deep down inside that you know and feel and nobody can take away from you.

Quentin charges ahead along the shortcut and we make our way down there too. It doesn't take long for us to get to the bottom of the logging trail, and soon we catch up with Quentin. From a short distance away we can see the back of one of the Bailey brothers working his way through the woods. Quentin makes a gurgling sound like a giggle being stepped on, and Conrad swats at the air. He rolls up his sleeves and turns around and puts a finger on his lips and goes, "Hush."

Frank or Fred Bailey is wearing green pants and a checkered shirt, and for someone in his early eighties, he's moving pretty fast. Soon enough we see him break out into the field and head toward the metal object on wheels that is sitting smack in the center. Tiny's there too wearing those greasy coveralls, and his big old hands are just pure grease up to his elbows.

A lot of the machine is wrapped up in that big blue flapping tarp. Mr. Bailey gets down on his back and slides under the tarp. Then Tiny stands there for the longest time waiting for his great-uncle to come back out. After a while Tiny starts kind of looking for him, poking his head here and there. Finally Mr. Bailey emerges from another area altogether. Tiny looks kind of surprised. We can't hear anything 'cause their words are carried away in the high wind that always seems to be down here in this field.

Quentin Duster flops back into the ferns, slapping his forehead. "Oh, man," he says, knocking off his glasses by mistake. Conrad rolls his sleeves up another notch and sits down next to Quentin. He picks up Quentin's glasses and puts them on and makes a studious-looking face. Then Quentin grabs the glasses back, whispering, "Cut it out."

We can't hear them out there, but they are still talking. Mr. Bailey gets up and walks around the machine, pointing out this and pointing out that. Then he pats Tiny on the back. Tiny smiles a great big smile, and we can see from here where Jimmy Leroy punched out Tiny's front tooth the day Tiny Bailey beat him at the Junior Tractor Pull up at the fair last year.

The wind blows and sings and whispers in the trees above. It's like watching a silent movie. I keep wishing Granddaddy's Zorro would drop down out of the trees in his black hat and black mask and draw a big Z with his sword on the side of Tiny's mysterious machine and clear up all the questions that are hovering around our heads like mosquitoes.

Now Mr. Bailey walks to the other side of the field, waves to Tiny, and then he disappears down the path.

Quentin Duster looks over at us and he's chewing on his lower lip. "There's something cooking. It's the Clark in me that knows. I can just feel it. The Clark in me says something's steaming on the stove."

"Well, the Lewis in me says you're stepping on my one good foot," says Conrad. "Move over."

"Oops, sorry," says Quentin. "Come on, Conrad, put two and two together. The whole Bailey family is in this up to their ears."

"Could be," says Conrad, weighing things in his mind the way he does. "It's true even though those Bailey brothers are old as the hills, they can be pretty wild at times. And one of them gets in trouble for speeding now and again. I see it in the local police column in the newspaper."

Yeah, I'm thinking as I hear that, I read that column too. It usually has stuff in it like *July 12th police responded to a call from a resident on Pleasant Street who said someone was stomping on her irises. Or July 14th police received a call from a woman on Belcher Street who said her husband was intoxicated and was up on the roof and wouldn't come down.*

"Something's cooking," says Quentin again. "Like I said, something's steaming on the stove right smack in front of us."

Me, I start thinking again about my house up in the field and how I've seen stuff there like cards and soda cans and suddenly I realize the Bailey brothers and Tiny are the ones who have been up at that house. And there was a fourth can of soda up there too, and it was a Dr. Pepper.

chapter 15

It's the first cold spring day we've had. The sky is a
miserable dark gray and everybody's half freezing. Still
the sidewalks are packed with people. There are forty-
some All-State marching bands dressed up in golds and
silvers with hats and batons all backed up behind the
firehouse. You can see them up there, overflowing like
a river pushing at the shore, waiting for the sound of
the cymbals, waiting to start the parade.

Conrad and I are sitting on the curb in front of
Bailey's Hardware to watch. Behind Conrad in the window of Bailey's Hardware there's a display of rakes and
shovels and there's a flowerpot with tulips growing in
it and a little sign that says, THE YEAR IN TULIPS AT
BAILEY'S HARDWARE. TULIPS IN FLOWERPOTS NOW!
COMING THIS FALL . . . 5,000 TULIP BULBS ON SALE!!!

The Bailey brothers have set two folding chairs up in the window and the two of them are sitting in there, smiling and waving from their warm spot. They do that for every parade we have in town except on Memorial Day, 'cause they both march in that parade wearing their old soldiers' uniforms.

I am looking up at those Bailey brothers sitting there with sack lunches and napkins on their laps and I'm hoping something they do will give me some kind of answer. Conrad too keeps his eyes right on them, watching one Bailey brother offer the other a nice big handful of potato chips.

Now we hear the loud cymbals clashing. The All-State parade is starting and the bands are being released into the street from the firehouse parking lot. First off, the Orkney Springs Regional comes marching down Main Street with a big yellow banner. They're wearing purple-and-yellow polyester pants and jackets with little gold flaps on the shoulders and they're in perfect step. Rows and rows of instruments file by, kids tooting all kinds of horns and hitting all kinds of drums. They're playing "Are You from Dixie?" and they sound pretty good. Conrad and I start tapping our feet and Conrad's all smiles.

Next a band comes through wearing fancy green velvet outfits with silver buttons and tassels on their hats. There's a kid carrying a sign that says CULPEPPER COMMUNITY MIDDLE SCHOOL, HOME TO THE CULPEP-PER COYOTES. Conrad looks at me and beams and then he looks away.

Most of the bands are wearing uniforms in their school colors. Mama said to me last night, "Our library board doesn't want to fix the library steps this year. Cheap old buzzards. Now when you see those marching bands tomorrow, you'll be able to tell by the quality of uniform which school boards are tight as misers."

Conrad and I are sitting here whistling away even though it's freezing cold out. Some of the bands as they march through are really good, almost to take my breath away, and some are just squeaking by, getting all out of step and all out of tune and moaning and mooing like a herd of infected cattle. There are so many bands, they just keep pouring down the street. Just when I think it's over and there can't be more, I hear another trumpet, another trombone, and I see another spiffy group popping along.

After a drum corps from Charlottesville thunders by, I look up and here comes the Cabanash County Elementary School Band, marching right past the Knights of Columbus Hall and heading toward us. Mr. Muzzle must have decided to go with a Blues Brothers theme 'cause everybody is wearing flashy sunglasses. Some kids have on crazy-looking wigs. Some are wearing bright-colored way-cool outfits like Billy Guffy, who is hitting a triangle and wearing a kind of fur-trimmed orange bathrobe and an orange curly wig. I look over at Conrad and his face has turned dark, like some kind of invisible baseball cap is throwing shadows over his eyes.

Next the flute and piccolo players march through, moving like one unit. Then the fourteen trombone players come sliding by, sliding out of tune and looking guilty. Right behind them is the flaky fourth grader with braids, twirling a baton and wearing a black felt Blues Brothers hat and sunglasses too.

The crowd goes wild not just 'cause they are the grade-school hometown band but because they have something going on that nobody else thought of, a kind of colorful flair that makes up for all the bad notes.

It is Quentin Duster's moment of glory. He is so small under that big old tuba you can barely see his little bobbing head. He's wearing clip-on sunglasses and a big wide wacky necktie. Right next to him is Tiny Bailey, the biggest Blues Brother you ever saw *boom boom boom*ing along. I can't help but notice his jumbo shoes keeping right in step.

I heard Mr. Muzzle had to do some fancy footwork over at the Vocational Center to get Tiny included in our band. Tiny seems to make Quentin look smaller, while Quentin makes Tiny look even bigger. Quentin's got some kind of look running across his face when he glances over at us, like he has something important in his upper left pocket.

"Looks like Quentin and Tiny are tight as a drum," says Conrad. "No pun intended."

"Yeah," I say, "and I bet we're gonna have to hang Quentin up by his ankles to get him to share what he knows."

At the back of the band is Mr. Muzzle. His feet are keeping the rhythm, but his face looks worn-out and his hair is all frazzled. I don't mean average tired. I mean he looks like somebody recently went over him with a street-cleaning machine.

After the parade, Cabanash County Elementary School Band doesn't place in any category at all, but Conrad seems a little quiet, standing around kicking the curb gently with the edge of his leg brace.

A lot of kids from the band have been hanging out in the street afterward, and Brice Buttonwood just came up and invited everyone standing there, except for Conrad and me, to Buttonwood's Bowl-a-rama just off Main Street for his sister's birthday after the parade. Conrad stood there like a sturdy old house in a storm, not moving, not showing anything until they were gone, and then he looked down at the curb. All the popular kids are so excited about the new Buttonwood's Bowl-a-rama coming to the shopping mall soon 'cause it's gonna have glow-in-the-dark bowling pins, glow-in-the-dark bowling balls, and glow-in-the-dark bowling shoes.

Billy Guffy has been running around in his great loose flapping orange bathrobe, chasing Quentin

Duster under the bleachers in the presentation area and then out along the parking lot. Quentin provoked it in the first place by stealing Billy Guffy's curly orange wig and wearing it backwards. Now Billy Guffy's mama just showed up in her car and she's beeping the horn, and Quentin looks all sheepish and takes the wig off and throws it to Billy Guffy.

Conrad and I move over toward the bleachers and we see Tiny Bailey sitting there eating a supersize sandwich all by himself. He's got his nice big feet propped up and he's sitting there chewing away. Quentin goes over to him, puts his hands on his hips, and says, "Nice job, Tiny." Tiny doesn't answer. He takes a bite of his sandwich. "I mean you whaled away at that drum and never missed a beat," says Quentin, shaking his head back and forth. Tiny takes another bite of his sandwich.

Finally Tiny says real slowly, "Well, did you ask him?"

"Uh, no, but can do," says Quentin, "can do, Tiny. Conrad, your mama still want to get rid of that big mess of T-shirts nobody wants?"

"Maybe," says Conrad. "You mean the ones that say *Best Things in Life Aren't Things*? People don't buy them.

They pass right over them. She's thinking of throwing them out or donating them."

"Well, tell her to donate them to me," says Tiny, throwing the last of his sandwich into the dark cave of his open mouth.

"What for?" says Conrad.

Tiny doesn't answer. Quentin looks at Conrad and I look at Quentin. Quentin's eyes go all big like two eggs frying in a pan and he says, "Well, I imagine your mama would be more than pleased to donate those old shirts, Conrad. What do you say?" Then Quentin elbows Conrad and Conrad elbows Quentin back. And they start punching each other and kicking.

Tiny balls up his sandwich paper and gets up, the biggest fifth-year senior you ever saw, and heads off toward town calling out, "Think it over. Let me know, Duster."

We're left sitting here on the bleachers with everybody just about cleared out, leaving a lot of paper cups and candy wrappers here and there on the ground. Quentin looks extra hopped up. He gets out his little All-State Pennant that everybody in the band got as a thank-you and he waves it around in the air and he says, "You should have seen that popcorn we had afterwards, Conrad. Somebody put food coloring in it and it was all red, white, and blue and swimming in butter. Best popcorn I ever had."

Conrad looks over at that little pennant and his face has a round yearning look to it like he's full up with Granddaddy's word *wistful*. He looks at that little old three-colored plastic pennant like he is thirsty on a desert island and seeing a glass of water floating in the distance.

So I say, "Hey, Conrad, just keep on renting that old saxophone. Come back next year so good everybody will freeze dead in their tracks. And anyway they got ice cream up at Mister Softee right now that's only fifty cents a cone. Let's go up there and suck up at least two apiece."

And that's what we do. And the whole way there I'm thinking how sweet it is that Conrad hasn't mentioned anything about any doctor or any impending operation today. And how for my part quitting band didn't matter at all. I didn't mind giving up that stupid trumpet. I just liked sitting with Conrad on the curb watching all those bands go by. For me there was no more perfect seat in the whole world. A fancy red velvet chair at the Grand Ole Opry that Mama always talks about couldn't have been any better, far as I'm concerned.

When I get home Mama has her head under the kitchen counter and Granddaddy's leaning over her and they're arguing about what went down the drain that shouldn't have. Mama gets up off her knees and wipes her hands on her apron and says, "Jessie Lou, I looked for you earlier in the trumpet section when your band marched by and I didn't see you. And where's your trumpet case today?"

"Oh, I quit band last week," I say, opening the fridge and grabbing a handful of leftover Tater Tots.

A look of light and joy passes across Mama's face.

"Honey," she says, running a wet dishrag over the counter, "why don't you try taking up the harp next time? It has such a delicate, pretty little sound."

Then Granddaddy starts hitting the drainpipe with a little hammer making a ferocious racket, and Mama sticks her head back under the counter and they start arguing again.

So I just head for the stairs. Before long, I'm lying on my bed looking at the moon that appears to be lost and confused in a sea of moving clouds. Soon enough through the walls I can hear Granddaddy's radio blaring away. He's already listening to a call-in talk show like he always does. The program is discussing the question, "If aliens ever land on our native soil, should the government tell everybody or keep it quiet?"

People are calling in to the radio show with their point of view about space aliens. Granddaddy called in one time on one of those talk shows, but he went on too long and he had to be cut off midway through a sentence. "Thank you, Mr. Ferguson," they said before Granddaddy had a chance to get his point across.

Melinda's room is on the other side of me opposite from Granddaddy's room. She's got an old Patsy Cline CD playing. Patsy Cline is Mama's favorite singer in the whole world and now Melinda likes her too. Melinda loves the song "Crazy," and she's probably trying to glue on those fake fingernails she bought in Charlottesville. I'm lying between both noises that become gibberish when mixed together, like Patsy Cline Meets the Space Aliens.

Too bad my sister decided to love the same music as my mama 'cause country music drives Granddaddy crazy. He used to wear earmuffs around the house every time Mama had a country song playing. Granddaddy calls that stuff cornball garbage. Me, I like country songs. They're kind of sad and have the sound of poetry about them, like one of my poems set to music.

"Okay, folks, what would you do if an alien walked into your front yard? Call us at 555-3452. Hello, you're on Ted's Talk Time."

I don't mean to feel grateful for what happened to Conrad's leg, and I wish I could say I want it fixed. But if it does get fixed, he won't need my help anymore. He'll get so popular he won't need anything. I wish, oh I wish, I wasn't so terrible awful. I pull off all the new scabs on my legs so they're rough and miserable-looking, so my knees will be sure to be covered in little white scars, so I'll have to wrap myself in darkness when I grow up.

And I don't feel sleepy at all and I wish I could get up and run down the road in the night and sit on the porch at the old house. Then I could look up and see every star in the sky and I could really imagine how Lewis and Clark could find their way by just looking at the heavens. It's nice to think those stars are so regular and so reliable. It's nice to think you could find your way in the dark wilderness by looking up above you at what is always there but hardly noticed.

chapter 16

At school we have a half hour just before lunch when everybody's supposed to work on their discovery reports. Mrs. Duster walks around the room, looking over everybody's shoulder and waving her arms here and there like she's conducting an orchestra. It makes me sorely uneasy that I haven't committed anything to paper at all. You'd expect something like that of Quentin Duster, but me, I usually have my work done and I'm reading some book at the back of the room while I'm waiting for everybody to catch up. My mama used to introduce me to her friends by saying, "And this is Jessie Lou, my reader." But I swear I haven't cracked open a book since we started this crazy project.

Quentin Duster saw Tiny Bailey up at Larry's Laundromat last night. Tiny was doing his own laundry, and Quentin was up there 'cause his cousin works the evening shift. Quentin knew right away Tiny was the guy unloading the dryer next to him when one of Tiny's giant mail-away socks fell out on the floor by Quentin's feet. And Tiny said right then to Quentin, "Got an answer about those T-shirts?" We couldn't get anything more out of Quentin about what else was said. All Quentin would tell us was that Tiny's coveralls still looked just as greasy coming out of the washing machine as going in.

Brice Buttonwood is almost done with his discovery report and he's up at the popular table acting way cool. He's got Tiffany B. holding a box of jumping crickets and they're making a chart that shows the length of each hop of each cricket and they're trying to show how if you feed a cricket this sugar water it jumps farther than the other crickets. Brice Buttonwood and Jenny Bonners and Tiffany B. are laughing and writing stuff down, and when Conrad goes over to see what they're doing, they get kind of quiet. They don't tear him to pieces like I've seen them do to some, but they just get sort of bored and kind of look through him like he's a screen door.

Still, Conrad seems to be chipper. He makes a few jokes, throws his pencil up in the air and catches it, and then goes back to look at his drawing from a standing angle. Now I can see the little fourth-grade girl with the braids and the squeaky voice going up to Conrad to tell him about the new cat she got from her aunt. She's not stopping there either. She's going on to explain who owned the cat before and why she likes the cat and all the names she's thinking over. Conrad just keeps smiling and nodding and listening to her while he works on his drawing of an amazing robot with blinking lights on the paper in front of him.

I look around me at everybody working away on their projects. I look at my teacher, who seems to be spinning and weaving and coaxing the air in front of each one of us. I think the time has come to tell Conrad and Quentin about the playing cards and the cans of soda up at the house. I think it's time to tell them we should go up there and poke around.

We get out early today. The teacher wants us to go to the library and work on our research. Quentin's all excited about the early release and flies down the hall and out the door like a loose cannon. (Those are my mama's words for Quentin. She goes, "That Quentin Duster's a loose cannon." But then she says that about a lot of people.) Conrad seems lighthearted and breezy about everything today. But me, I'm thinking, *What do we do at the library? We haven't got anything to look up yet.* Quentin's kind of strutting ahead of us and then turning around looking important.

We get outside the library, and Quentin stands there looking up at us, squinting through his glasses. Conrad says, "What?"

And Quentin says, "Took care of that problem."

"What problem, Quentin?" I say. Quentin reaches in his backpack and pulls out an old wrinkled index card that says on it, *Quentin Duster, library file.* Dinosaur Days of Yore *checked out April 23, 2004.* OVERDUE. *FINE OWED.* Somebody has written on the card, *Mr. Duster is not allowed to check out books until this fine is taken care of and the book is returned.*

"It's my file, my library record, my index card, shows what I took out and what I owe," says Quentin.

"Give me that thing," says Conrad, grabbing the card. "*Dinosaur Days of Yore* ... Quentin, that book is 730 days overdue! You owe big-time. Where did you get this card anyway?"

"Never mind where I got it," says Quentin, snatching the card back. "Just let's see what I'm going to *do* with it." And he holds the index card out in front of him and he rips it into tiny pieces. Lets it blow all over the road. "That's the end of that," he says, brushing off his hands. "I'm not paying a fine like that for *Dinosaur Days of Yore*. At twenty-five cents a day for 730 days, I owe almost two hundred dollars, and I'm not paying two hundred dollars for a book that isn't even worth two cents."

Conrad shrugs his shoulders. "Well, Quentin, it's up to you. What are you going do when they find out your index card is missing?"

"They won't know. They'll just think I never existed." Quentin says.

"Then who are they going to think is playing Pac-Man in there all the time?" I say.

"I'm going to tell them my name is Chester Winslow

if they ask. Remember that kid who moved here for two months last year? That'll put the whole matter to rest," says Quentin.

Brice Buttonwood, Tiffany B., and Jenny Bonners are lounging on the steps of the library, reminding me of a family of lazy lions stretched out on the cement terrain at the Roanoke Zoo. Conrad looks over at them and kind of partway smiles.

"I saw some stuff up at that old lonesome house. Some stuff that might be helpful," I say, rolling my eyes from Conrad to Brice and back.

Quentin's doing a combination of karate and kick-boxing with an invisible opponent on the sidewalk. Every time he throws a kick or a punch at the sky, he looks out of the corner of his eyes up at the popular kids on the steps.

"Come on," I say again, "let's go over to that house. I saw a bunch of stuff there."

"Oh, yeah? Like what?" says Quentin, kicking the air.

"Like trust me," I say, feeling like Sacagawea herself even though I didn't get the part. Then I think about Sacagawea running along through the woods with a papoose on her back. Did the baby cry or did it just ride along in silence?

I take off down the street and Quentin and Conrad follow. Soon enough we get on the dirt road that goes along the Cabanash River, and before you know it we're almost to the house in the fields.

The green this time of year is almost to be lime green. The grass so new and tender and so green as to almost make you cry. Then you hear those red-winged blackbirds and the bobwhites in the field and it's so sweet and new as almost to feel like anguish itself. I've quit writing any more poems about spring. (I have tons.) Everybody tries and nobody can get close to the way it feels when the grass is in its green early childhood and most of the trees are still bare. It's just pure beautiful anguish.

Conrad goes up on the silvery weathered porch and leans against one of the windows, looking in. Quentin follows him, leaving muddy footsteps behind him and making a lot of noise. Through the window the rooms look so undisturbed. More than quiet. It's a *silence*. As if everything is stopped still and waiting for something.

"So what did you see?" Conrad whispers, getting steamy breath on the windowpane. It condenses and Quentin draws a Pac-Man smile in the condensation.

I want to tell them how I feel about this house. Like it's mine. I remember a while ago it was all boarded up. I remember seeing the wind and rain howling around it in the wintertime. I could almost see someone wrapping their arms around the house, looking for a way in. Now it's opened up again, but it still has an empty gone boarded-up lonely feel. "See those cans of soda in there? And a few days ago there were playing cards, but they're gone now," I say.

"Meaning what?" says Quentin.

"Meaning this," says Conrad, turning the handle on the door and pushing it slowly open.

"This might be a lame idea, Conrad," says Quentin and then he looks startled, slaps his forehead, and goes, "Sorry, Conrad, didn't mean it like that."

"It's okay, lamebrain," says Conrad, "hush now." Conrad's the only boy in Cabanash County who uses the word *hush*, and when he says it, his voice is warm and coaxing, making you *hush, hush, hush* deep down.

Once inside the house, the cleanness and quietness soothes me. Even though I'm nervous 'cause I know we shouldn't be in here, there's a peaceful feeling coming from the floorboards. A calm order. All this time I've known this house from the outside only. I've never been inside. Now I'm inside looking out at the old maple tree in the front yard, at the windy fields across the road. It looks so different being inside looking out instead of outside looking in. It's a whole new view of everything.

The house has old furniture in it, fabric at the windows in back from some other time, and dishes too that look like they're from even before Mama was born. When I open the closet door in the plain quiet bedroom, there are old dresses and coats in there like what people wore around the time of World War II. It feels strange and at the same time it feels familiar, like I know it already. Conrad and Quentin are sitting around throwing cards at each other that they found in a little box on the table, and I go to the window to watch the wind moving the grass.

"Hey, somebody want a soda?" says Quentin, holding up a can of Dr. Pepper. I turn around to look at what he's holding up and I see right behind him one of the Day-Glo orange vests everybody wore on the senior citizens' walkathon last week, hanging over the back of a chair, and there's a huge pair of work boots in the corner. But I'm not gonna say anything. Not yet anyway.

Quentin's trying on the boots still in his own shoes and he's clumping around making dumb jokes, and Conrad's lying on the daybed with his arms up behind his head just taking it easy.

Then Quentin ups and says, "Hey, Conrad, what'd you think of Moon n' Stars Montgomery's drawing of a horse today? She draws good, doesn't she? Horses are hard, aren't they?"

"Yep," says Conrad.

"You like her?" says Quentin. "Come on, admit it. You want to marry her."

Before you know it, Conrad's tackling Quentin again and they're punching each other and knocking stuff over and then soon enough it turns into a bullfighting game where Conrad's holding up a red cloth that was lying on a chair and Quentin's being a bull and charging at it and they're carrying on like two idiots, so

I just go in the kitchen and stand at the old sink and wonder who lived here.

I just stand here full of awe. I turn the old faucet on and let rusty water run over my hands. Looks to me like this house hasn't been used much in fifty years or more. Feels like it's just waiting for someone to come back, to pull up along the road in an old pickup.

In a matter of seconds through the window I see Tiny Bailey coming up into the lower yard with his big old Vocational Center tool kit in hand. He would be hard to miss, being six foot something and weighing in at who knows what. His great big T-shirt says *Junior Tractor Pull, Shenandoah State Fair.* I can just see Tiny at the tractor pull last year growling and shouting and gunning that motor on his tractor as they loaded on more and more weights in the back, till his tractor tires gutted out deep trenches in the mud and the tractor slid sideways and backwards. Still they kept putting on more weights.

"Tiny's in the yard," I say.

"Quick," says Conrad, "get under the bed."

"I'll take notes," says Quentin, ripping a piece of paper out of a notebook and stuffing it in his pocket.

My heart starts thumping like a bumper car at the state fair, and Quentin rolls under the bed. Conrad pushes in after him and I squeeze in at the end, holding my breath, then letting it out slowly, so I won't make a sound. Now I'm lying in the dark, looking up at a bunch of broken-down old bedsprings and listening for footsteps, but I don't hear any.

"Conrad," whispers Quentin, "is this what they call breaking and entering? We could end up at Weeks School making leather wallets."

"Hush," says Conrad again, "not a sound."

We are lying here like sardines in a can. And Quentin's all wiggly and breathing loud, and I bet as soon as Tiny steps foot in this house, he'll pull Quentin out from under here like a rabbit out of a hat.

"Maybe he's not coming in," says Conrad, rolling his eyes over toward me. I am looking at Conrad's face, how the shadows change it. He has two dimples, one on either cheek, so he always looks like he's about to laugh, but now I can see clearer the little indentation on his chin. Is it called a cleft? I haven't seen Conrad in the dark like this before. It's like seeing him for the first time all over again.

"How old do you have to be before they send you up to Weeks School?" says Quentin.

If I were to die under this bed, I am thinking it would be about the best way to go, scrunched up so close to Conrad I can breathe in his very essence. Up close Conrad smells what I can only describe as *popular*. What I mean by that is, I smell a T-shirt fresh out of the dryer, warm right down to its fibers with a memory of soap hovering around it. There's an air around that T-shirt that says *nothing* matters 'cause you know who you are, where you're going, and what you're gonna do.

"What's the age limit up there?" says Quentin again.

But I don't answer. I'm breathing the deep down popular air that surrounds Conrad Parker Smith. No matter whether Brice Buttonwood looks through him like a broken screen door or not. No matter whether every popular kid in the class goes to some party and Conrad doesn't get invited. 'Cause you just can't take it away from Conrad. You just can't.

And I am thinking to be a sardine right now with Conrad Parker Smith is the closest thing to heaven. Except for Quentin. He is looking crabby and like he's about to swat somebody and shout out, "Move over, turkey!" We lie under those old crazy-looking bedsprings for going on five minutes and there's no sign of Tiny and there's nothing to take notes on.

Finally Quentin rolls out and looks around and says, "Tiny disappeared. Vanished. Now how does a great big teen like that just disappear?"

"What are you in such a big hurry for, Quentin? Looking to stop off at Moon n' Stars's house and give her a kiss?" says Conrad, standing up and brushing the dust off his sleeves.

"I'll leave that to you, Conrad," says Quentin. "I gotta get home. I got four cousins coming up from Memphis, Tennessee, today. And if I'm not there, they all go after my dinosaurs. The five-year-old they call the 'Holy Terror' usually leaves nothing but dust in his wake."

I'm the last one to get out from under the bed and as I'm lying here alone, I see right there stuck in the molding along the wall is a piece of paper. I pull it out but it's only an old envelope, says on the outside of it *To Vera Bailey*, and there's a stamp on it with a postmark from 1940. I put the envelope in my pocket and then I roll out from under the bed. Quentin makes a dumb joke about me being like a skinny rolling pin, which I ignore.

We go to the door of the old house and as we're leaving, I take one more look at my granddaddy's Day-Glo vest hanging over the chair. Then we're out in the yard.

Two seconds later we think we see Tiny's overgrown shadow stomping behind the bushes and we make a run for the barn. The big doors are open, and we kind of dive in and roll along the hay on the floor. We lie there flat out for a while settling into the darkness of the barn, our eyes slowly growing accustomed to the velvet black air.

I can hear coyotes shrieking across the road down in the swamp. Like I said before, we have a whole lot of coyotes around here and people like to hunt them, going in big lines cornering them, cutting them off like an army, and then shooting them. But there's so many they can't seem to get them all. They say coyotes don't bother people, but their howl is the wildest loneliest sound I ever heard. It's such a mournful screaming coming up out of the swamp, calling their mama, calling their daddy, screaming, "Take me out of this world, nobody loves me, nobody wants me. Oh, lonely, lonely, lonely me."

Now our eyes are used to the darkness and we look around the barn. There are four empty horse stalls and a loft full of old sagging hay. A bird lets loose in the darkness, sings a few notes, and we look up, up toward the pitched tall ceiling. There in the high rafters we can see something shiny. Two huge glistening aluminum metal things hidden up there high in the rafters. They are so big as to take your breath away, spanning the whole width of the barn. They are so polished, every rivet tight, every bolt oiled.

"Well," says Conrad, "just look at that."

"What?" says Quentin. "What is it?"

"Airplane wings. Those are the wings to an airplane. Wings to an old 1930s barnstormer," says Conrad. "I did a bunch of drawings of old airplanes last month. Looks just like one I drew."

"Is that what Tiny's been fixing up?" I say. Conrad leans his head back and looks up, like he can handle anything, making me feel like pure girl, all protected in his know-how.

"Yep," says Conrad. "Looks like Tiny's fixing up that old airplane in secret, like somebody's planning to fly somewhere."

When we scramble on our hands and knees out of the barn and make it up to the road, Quentin says, "I know this sounds spooky but I feel honestly like Clark is with me. I feel like I am really becoming him, now that we've finally made a true discovery." Then he makes like he's a ghost waving his arms and he takes off after me trying to scare me, and we waver and hover down the road at Conrad's pace like three spooks.

When we get to my house about a quarter mile farther, it's all lit up, glowing orange in the dark windy night. I stand on the porch and wave to Conrad and Quentin. I watch them sail over the hill like two dark little boats. Then I go in the house knowing I've missed dinner.

As soon as I hit the door, I can smell the Martha Nottingham shepherd's pie. With that mix, all you do is add hamburger and a package of frozen vegetables, stick it in the oven, and you've got a like-to-die shepherd's pie. The house smells so good and it's warm and Granddaddy and Mama and Melinda are in the sitting room. Melinda is practicing reciting the poem I've loaned her. It's the one called "Big Old Lazy River." And she is repeating the line "The river's long and lazy."

Mama is saying "Melinda, put your emphasis on the word *long*. Draw the word out so it sounds long: *The river's LONG and lazy*."

It is odd to hear my mama reciting a line from a poem of mine. She thinks it's Melinda's poem, which is fine with me. She doesn't even know I write poems. Nobody knows I write poems. I didn't even know Melinda knew. I don't write them for anybody to read anyway. I just write them to write them.

Granddaddy is asleep in the La-Z-Boy recliner. He's always asleep in that recliner. He never believes that he actually falls asleep in that chair, always says he doesn't. So I took a picture of him sleeping one time with his digital camera. "Now do you believe me, Granddaddy?" I said to him, showing him the photograph. "You sleep in that chair all the time."

"I wasn't asleep, Jessie Lou. I was just resting my eyes," he said.

Tonight I go in the kitchen and get a bowl of shepherd's pie and I climb the stairs with it, hearing Melinda reciting my poem over and over again. "'Big Old Lazy River' by Melinda Ferguson," she says as I hit the top stair.

By the time I get to my room, it's starting to storm again. The black rain is pelting against the glass and our house is shaking in the wind. I sit at my little desk for a minute and get out my writing pad that my granddaddy gave me that says on the top *From the Desk of Jessie Lou Ferguson*. Then I put the pad back in the drawer because I don't have that tingly feeling telling me a poem is on the way.

It's getting late, and Melinda just came upstairs and went to bed. I can tell it's her by the way she slammed the door. I'm waiting for Mama to go to sleep now, so I can go downstairs. Usually she watches late-night TV reruns of *Decorate with Suzi Anne*, a program that shows you how to decorate your old crummy house and turn it into a palace with almost no money.

I wait till Mama's light goes out and then I slip downstairs and sit by my granddaddy at the kitchen table where he's doing another jigsaw puzzle of a president. (He frames all the presidents when he's done and hangs them up in the living room.)

I lean my head against Granddaddy and watch him put in part of Jimmy Carter's eyebrows. Then I turn over some of the puzzle pieces for him, looking for dark brown sections of Jimmy Carter's suit.

"Sugar pie, you need to be sawing wood right now. Why don't you go on up to bed," says Granddaddy.

"Granddaddy," I say. "What do you suppose Tiny Bailey's working on a 1930s airplane for?"

Granddaddy looks at me for a while with his nice old granddaddy eyes that remind me of that special soft blue chalk up at Bailey's Hardware.

He keeps on looking at me and finally he says, "Well, sugar pie, you've played Monopoly before. What do you think happens? You get one big fat winner and everybody else starves. It isn't that different here in West Taluka Falls. What do you think is gonna happen to the Bailey Brothers' Hardware when that great big superchain hardware store opens up?"

"Don't know, Granddaddy," I say.

"Well, I'll tell you what's gonna happen. Nobody's gonna shop there anymore. So we gotta fight back a little. You can keep a secret, can't you, Jessie Lou?"

"You know I can, Granddaddy," I say.

"Well, old Frank Bailey's gonna surprise everybody by flying that plane during the big air show that's coming up for the opening-day celebration of the shopping mall. He's gonna pull a big banner across the sky for Bailey's Hardware. We don't want people to forget the store that's been here fifty years. Do we, sugar pie?" Granddaddy looks sad, and when he does, the blue in his eyes goes gray and shimmers like water.

"Granddaddy," I say, "is it a mean old world?"

"Yes and no," says Granddaddy, putting in a white flower on Jimmy Carter's lapel. "Yes and no, sugar pie."

chapter 17

Next few days, it continues to rain. The Cabanash River near our house has swollen up big and fat. Cows are standing in fields of water. Our driveway has grown muddy. And we're looking at the spring state fair coming up by the end of the week. I can't imagine them putting up their tents in all this rain. I don't know how they will set up all those rides.

Mama says Granddaddy's the only old man in the state of Virginia who likes to ride on the Screamin' Demon with all those teenagers who don't have any sense of danger. I'll ride with him on *most* of the rides but not all of them. Granddaddy likes the Sky Bullet the best, and I won't go with him on that one 'cause they say it's so mean and scary you throw up and your throw-up flies back around and hits you in the face. Everybody's looking forward to the fair for different reasons. If I get a chance, I'm going to try to get myself hypnotized, find out if I was a dog or a bird in my past life.

By the opening day of the fair, the rain hasn't subsided at all. I know Conrad and Quentin are getting to go up there together tonight. I am miserable jealous about that 'cause I know I have to go with Mama and Melinda and Granddaddy to make a family presentation. When you win something like a Junior Teen Beauty Pageant, your whole family gets involved. "It isn't anything anybody ever does alone," says Mama. "It's a whole group of people behind somebody. It's a group effort."

This afternoon Mama is in the kitchen ironing Melinda's dress and slips. "She's just a little doll," Mama says. "Isn't she sweet?"

"Pretty as a picture," says Granddaddy, counting his dollar bills on the table, separating out his state fair money, licking his fingers and peeling off another dollar bill.

"I don't think you'll be able to take Jessie Lou on any rides in this weather, Granddaddy," says Mama. "The radio's going on about flood warnings. I'm sure those rides will be out of commission. The wind and rain are too strong."

"They don't pack up those rides just 'cause of a few drops of rain," says Granddaddy.

Melinda comes downstairs wearing curlers and an old sweatshirt and holding her satin shoes. Those shoes lying there in her hands seem to glow, to emanate light, to shine like a pair of magic slippers from some other world. The glow from those shoes seems to light up Melinda's face. She's looking down like she's holding something so precious, something alive, like those slippers are two pink birds sleeping in her hands. "Granddaddy," she says, "Mama and I went over to Roanoke to get these shoes dyed professionally."

"I know that, sweetheart," says Granddaddy.

"Aren't they a pretty pink? Matches my dress exactly."

"Honey," says Mama, "they're salmon-colored, not pink. There's a big difference. Can't you see the warm tones and how they bring out the highlights in your cheeks?"

I'm lying on the couch already wearing my stupid blue-and-white-checked dress that Mama got me at

JCPenney. I hate it. It's too big for me and there's a white collar hanging down in front that looks like a bib.

"Jessie Lou, sweetie," says Mama. "You're getting your dress all wrinkled lying there."

"Who cares?" I say. "I don't think anybody's gonna die if they see an imperfection in this old thing that looks like a big tablecloth."

Granddaddy looks real nice though. He's all spiffed up wearing a new plaid shirt and a jacket. He's got his money folded neatly in his wallet. He's got big plans for him and me and the Sky Bullet and the Screamin' Demon. I'm not gonna do it. Love ya to pieces, Granddaddy, I'm thinking to myself, but I'm not going to get hit in the face with my own throw-up.

My feet are squeezed into these white plastic shoes, and it's still raining. Walls of it are melting against our windows. The living room feels hot and muffled. Melinda's all pinned back in her curlers and creams, pinned back like a bud before it blooms. If only I had Granddaddy's digital camera right now, I'd take a picture of her. She looks so awful, she reminds me of Quentin Duster that time he got a Mohawk haircut and totally fried his chances for popularity all in one swoop. "Granddaddy, where's your digital camera?" I say, looking over at Melinda and smiling.

She says, "Don't even think about it. Even done up like I am now, I'd still come out ahead of you."

"I would never be in a beauty contest," I say. "Be about a big waste of my time."

We can hear thunder in the distance and Mama says, "Sounds like it's over in Culpepper County."

"Yeah, we've had too much rain," says Granddaddy. "Either we don't get enough or we get too much."

I remember looking at the Cabanash River on the way home from school. It was big and fat and swollen, pressing at its edges, getting wider and greener with the rain falling in it. Rain hitting the surface of it, making little bubbles and knicks and splashes across it, trees bending over it, hanging down low and heavy, dancing and crying with rain.

Mama finishes Melinda's dress and lifts it off the ironing board and then slips it on a padded hanger. It's like a soft pink floating rose, gauzy like angel wings. The room smells sweet and smoky of freshly ironed fabric, pressed perfectly. Mama is good at ironing and sewing too, and once she entered an apron she made at the state fair in the Crafts Division. She took home a little old blue ribbon for it, though nobody made a fuss over it. You can still see that blue ribbon pinned to the wall above her dresser or maybe it isn't there anymore. It seems like we took it down and used it for some game we were playing back when Melinda and I used to be friends.

Everybody is finally all scrubbed and shiny like a set of spoons all done up with silver polish. Needless to say, Melinda looks like a princess out of a storybook in her salmon-colored angel slippers and matching gauzy angel-wing dress. All she lacks is a halo.

We have three umbrellas and when we run out to Mama's van, the rain is coming at us from all angles, blowing the yard around and mixing everything up. Granddaddy's lawn chair goes tumbling off down the road and Mama calls out, "Let that old hunk of junk go, Granddaddy. Get in the van."

Once we're inside the van with the rain hammering on us, Mama starts turning the key and the motor starts making that grinding growling no-way-José kind of noise. "I guess we'll have to take Granddaddy's car," says Mama.

"Told you," says Granddaddy, "these vans are no good."

"I can't show up in Granddaddy's ugly old car," says Melinda. "Everybody'll laugh at me." She looks like she is going to cry.

Mama says, "Don't you dare shed a tear, Melinda May. It'll ruin your makeup. Don't shed a tear till you win."

"I won't go in Granddaddy's car," says Melinda, crossing her arms.

"We have to get going, honey. It really doesn't matter how we get there, long as we get there," says Mama.

"Granddaddy drives too slow anyway," says Melinda.

"Now come on, little girl," says Granddaddy, "let your granddaddy take care of things. Don't get all upset, we'll get you there."

We make the dash from the van to the car all at once, umbrellas puffing up in the wind, feeling like to carry us away. Me, I step in a puddle, making my white plastic shoes feel cold and stiff and clammy. Granddaddy's car starts like a top. "What did I tell you, sugar pie," says Granddaddy, giving Melinda a special just-for-her kind of look. But she doesn't even see it. She's tapping her fists together, staring out the window, wearing a wet raincoat over her pink cloud dress, and it kind of spoils the effect like a coat will do on Halloween.

"You all in one piece, sweetheart?" says Mama, looking around smiling. "Where's all this rain coming from? Radio's going on all day about flash flooding this and flash flooding that and I've heard all kinds of crazy warnings in this county and that county. Where do you suppose it's all coming from?"

As we pull out of the driveway I am up on my knees looking out the back window at the river pushing at its edges. "What are you doing, Jessie Lou?" says Mama. "Sit down, honey. Stop jumping all around. Boy, if I could bottle whatever it is you've got that makes you so energetic, I'd be a rich woman. Wouldn't I, Granddaddy?"

"This car sounds like an old chain saw or a motorboat, Mama," says Melinda. The trees are heaving and flinging themselves back and forth along the road that follows the river.

"River's so full," says Mama. "Look how fast it's going!" Leaves and twigs and water and rain blow over the road. I lay my head back on the seat. It's been a while since anybody has mentioned any experiments or any half-cracked operations on poor old Conrad's leg. Maybe the whole notion will just drift away as hearsay and nonsense. And I'm wondering about those extra T-shirts Conrad's mother made, the ones Tiny Bailey wants. Now I know why he wants them.

We drive over the crest of the hill and down the road, going the back way past the silver-colored windswept house on the edge of the field, rain ripping across it, birds hidden away in the bushes around it. I kind of wonder where that vintage airplane came from and what exactly is an old barnstormer.

"We aren't late, are we?" says Melinda. "Drive faster, Granddaddy."

"Well, I can't go much faster, 'cause it's hard to see in all this rain," says Granddaddy. The windshield wipers are working overtime, going back and forth, back and forth. Going down the hill through the woods, we can hear the river roaring below.

Mama says, "That's almost too loud to be true. Hear that water? The river's cheering for you, Melinda!"

The sky seems to be getting darker. It's a charcoal-green smoky color and we can hear thunder drumming in the hills above us. Granddaddy clicks on his high beams. "Don't worry about this old car. She's a tank," says Granddaddy.

"What time is it?" says Melinda. "And sit back, Jessie Lou, I can't see around your big head."

More lightning. More rain. The car sails down the hill and at the bottom there is a stream running over the road, a wide, rushing stream. "Hold on," says Granddaddy. "We're going through it." And he guns the motor and the car sinks into the water and moves through it pretty quickly until the water seems to be rising and the wheels are spinning in the mud underneath. The motor sounds as if it's swallowing water and then it stops and Granddaddy can't get it going again.

"Mama!" Melinda calls. "Mama, we're stuck. And the water is rising, Granddaddy."

"Get out of the car!" shouts Granddaddy. "Grab those umbrellas. I'll carry you, Melinda. Hurry." Granddaddy is standing out in the water, a river running around his legs, thunder and lightning and rain everywhere, his face and hair all wet. "Hurry, sweetie, let me carry you. Jessie Lou, you hold on to Mama and you get across. Get on the other side and get under cover over there by the rock ledge. Go on."

I struggle to open the car door. Water is pushing against it, and when I finally get it open, water roars in on the floor all over my feet and ankles. I climb out into the water and work my way through it, holding Mama's hand. Her hair is all wet and the bottom of her skirt drags in the water.

Granddaddy carries Melinda gently, carefully, and she holds an umbrella over her head, crying and saying, "I can't help it, Mama, I have to cry." Granddaddy wades through the water that is rushing and rising around us, carrying Melinda, all the while making sure her butterfly pink dress doesn't dip and trail.

I get to the other side and I climb up the muddy rise and duck under a rocky ledge, followed by Mama and Melinda and Granddaddy. Then all of us are standing there, wet as dogs and muddy, except for Melinda. Granddaddy kept her pretty dry. We stand there waiting for the rain to subside.

Granddaddy's car is filling up with water. We can see it almost running over the seats. I can't help looking down at Melinda's shoes as we stand here. They are covered with mud and water spots. They look like somebody's been crying all over them.

"Don't worry," says Mama. "A car'll come along and give us a ride. We'll fix everything when we get there. We'll go in the ladies' room and get you all straightened out. They're expecting you, honey. Even if you are a little late, you've got a number. You're all registered. They won't start without you."

Mama has a knack for being right and she stays real level when everything seems to be falling apart. Like the time Granddaddy had a cookout for fourteen Lions Club members at the house. They left the steaks out on the picnic table while the grill was heating up. Then all the Lions Club members and Granddaddy went into the garage so Granddaddy could show off his new lawn mower. While they were in the garage, Bongo, the neighbors' big Saint Bernard, came over and ate all the steaks, every one of them, and all the potato salad too. It looked like the afternoon was going to be a disaster, but Mama was able to produce, on call, fifteen frozen hamburger patties from the fridge. So they cooked them up and all the Lions Club members were very cheerful and happy to be eating anything at all and Granddaddy's cookout was a huge success.

"That big dog eating the steaks was a subject for a great many jokes, while otherwise there might not have been anything to talk about at all. Helped make the event a success," Mama said later. I keep thinking about Granddaddy's cookout as we stand here, soaking wet, rain continuing without letting up.

Melinda is leaning against Granddaddy and he is saying, "Now, now, little girl, we've got plenty of time. Not to worry." Granddaddy's car is beginning to look like a big white hippopotamus sinking deeper into the mud and water.

Soon enough I hear another sound besides the rain, besides the river roaring. The sound of a motor. A gray SUV is coming down the hill. Granddaddy goes out into the road and starts waving his hands around, his white hair flying every which way. He's all wet and skinny-looking, my granddaddy. Makes him look frail, like a poor old tomcat that fell in a puddle of water. I can't stand to see my granddaddy look so old and windblown, so I bite my lip till it bleeds 'cause I want him to live forever.

The SUV comes sailing on down the hill, slides into the water covering the road, churns through it like a boat, and comes up on the other side, perky and full of pep. Granddaddy waves his arms like a windmill. The guy at the wheel stops his car, hits his automatic buttons, and his windows roll down. "Looks like you could use a lift and some help getting that old jalopy out of there."

"It's a Chrysler Imperial. Had it for thirty years. It's a good car. Usually runs like a top," calls Granddaddy through the wind and rain.

"Well, those things are low to the ground," the man shouts back. "Why don't you all get in and I'll give you a lift somewhere. I think you're off the road enough that people can get around you."

Mama looks at Melinda and Melinda looks at Mama and then they hug each other and kind of squeal. The guy pushes open the door to the backseat and we climb in, me hitching up my saggy soggy checkered dress and Melinda getting into the SUV like it is a golden carriage with a footman, looking at it amazed, like it had been a pumpkin just a half hour ago.

We roar off through the rain, following the gray-green swollen rushing river toward the spring state fair that's going on full blast in the distance in spite of the rain. "This is just so kind of you. My daughter Melinda is a contestant in the beauty contest over there. I always wanted to be in a beauty contest when I was a little girl. Never got a chance," says Mama, looking out the window.

Then Melinda nudges me with her elbow and mouths the words "Quit wiggling around so much. He's going to stop the car and throw us out."

And I say out loud, "No, he will not." And Melinda whisks her head around and stares out the window.

"Some kind of weather," says Granddaddy. "I sure hope I can get my old Imperial on out of the mud."

"You'll have to come back in the morning," says the man. "It'll clear up by then. It better had. I'll drop you folks off by the main pavilion." He turns onto a small dirt road, joining a muddy line of traffic on the grassy sloping field around the fair. "Ever been over to the hypnotist show? My wife and I went there last year and the fella chose me out of the crowd. He hypnotized me and he had me speaking fluent French. I tell you something right now, I never did take a foreign language in school and I don't know a word of anything but English."

When the SUV stops and it's time to get out, I'm so wet and cold that I feel like I'm not going to be able to uncurl and stand up like I'm supposed to. But I start to perk up when I hear all the music coming from those crazy rides and I see all those red, yellow, and green lights blinking away, full of all kinds of promise.

chapter 18

We spend about a half hour in the ladies' room hitting the hot air button on the hand dryer over and over again. I am holding my shoes and then my socks over the heat to dry them. Melinda goes "Pee-yew" when I hold up my socks. But they aren't old smelly socks, they're just *wet* socks. Mama gets her skirt kind of dry the same way and she fixes Melinda's hair and scrubs at the mud spots on her shoes. She smoothes out the netting on her dress and reapplies Melinda's Pink Parade lipstick.

Then we go on into the pavilion. Mama and Melinda go backstage and Granddaddy and I push into the fourth row where our name tags are attached to chairs. I can tell Granddaddy is feeling kind of important thinking that everybody is watching us because we're the family of Melinda Ferguson. Granddaddy's jacket is still wet and as we sit down, I notice his shoes are dark and soggy-looking.

While we're waiting for the pageant to begin, I see Fred and Frank Bailey are in the same row with their wives. I decide to look at both of them at the same time and I try to memorize their little differences. One seems to have heavier eyebrows but it's hard to keep track, and soon enough the lights are out. Rain is still coming down, rolling against the tin roof of the pavilion.

Now there's a man standing in a round circle of spotlight. "Good evening, ladies and gentlemen. We are going to start the Apple Blossom Junior Teen Beauty Pageant tonight with a talent show. Each of the twenty-five contestants has been asked to recite something they wrote, so we can hear the sound of their voices and see how they make a presentation."

As he is talking, I look around toward the back of the crowd and I can see Conrad and Quentin acting stupid, whispering and not paying attention. The man introduces the first ten contestants and each one comes out and recites something. Some read essays, some poems, and one girl reads part of a short story about a tree that can talk. I think it's really stupid. Quentin and Conrad do too, 'cause I can hear them giggling. There are a couple of babies crying in the back, covering up some of Conrad and Quentin's noise.

Then the announcer says, "Our next contestant is Melinda Ferguson. She is thirteen years old, and she is going to recite her poem called 'Big Old Lazy River.' Well, I don't know if any of you saw the Cabanash River down in the hollow tonight, but it didn't look too lazy to me." The crowd laughs and then the spotlight falls on my older sister, Melinda, coming out onstage looking like a nervous rose-colored princess.

I can see she's scared, but she stands still in the spotlight and then she says, "I'd like to read the poem 'Big Old Lazy River,' written by me, Melinda Ferguson." She takes a deep breath and then she begins to read.

> *Big old lazy river,*
> *Winding to the sea,*
> *Slow and sleepy river,*
> *Bring him back to me.*

The river's long and lazy
And I am young and free
People think I'm crazy.
Just bring him back to me.
Big old sleepy river,
I'm here on bended knee.
Put out your sails
And blow your wind
And bring him back to me.
Yes, bring him back to me.

The crowd is very quiet while Melinda says my poem, so quiet that if a feather should fall off a seagull's back right now and float right to the ground, you could hear it as it touches. A whisper kiss. I almost can't believe that everybody is listening to *my* poem. It's a secret poem that I wrote for Conrad Parker Smith. It was a secret from me to myself. I never would want Conrad to know I wrote such a thing for him. He'd probably turn green and die if he were ever to suspect.

There is a second right now where everyone is silent and the poem is finished. Then suddenly the crowd starts clapping and cheering. They go on and on. I look over at Granddaddy and he is clapping too. "Looks like they really liked Melinda's poem," he says, raising his bushy eyebrows and smiling.

They keep clapping and clapping. Then as Melinda slips offstage like a princess floating away, the announcer says, "That was a good poem, Melinda Ferguson. Thank you for sharing it with us."

The crowd claps some more and then the announcer starts talking about another girl named Stacey Pratt from Roanoke and how she is going to recite part of her fire prevention essay. "Miss Pratt wrote this essay for Fire Prevention Week this year," says the announcer.

The second part of the show, the announcer says, is the most important part, and it's based on pure beauty. "Now let's have all twenty-five young ladies out here so you can see all the contestants at once. Then we'll bring each one out individually. Now you in the audience can make the choice for yourself while our panel of judges up here to the left of me will cast their votes for third place, second place runner-up, *and* number one, the

Apple Blossom Junior Teen Beauty Queen!" The crowd cheers.

Then all the contestants come out and stand in a line onstage. For a minute I cannot find my big sister. Then there she is standing between two taller girls. In fact, everybody onstage seems taller and older and more at ease than Melinda. Suddenly she looks so small and the spotlights seem to be hitting her in the face. It looks to me like at any moment she might burst into tears. I can see a faint tracing of a water stain on the netting over her dress.

"Granddaddy," I whisper, "is Melinda short?"

"Well, I'll tell you something, if you're friends with one of the judges, *that's* how you win," says Granddaddy. "Those judges will pick their friends or the daughters of their friends. That's how everything works."

"What about being the prettiest?" I say.

"You think they pick the winner on beauty and merit? Bah," says Granddaddy. "You could be the most beautiful girl in the world, and if you didn't have a friend on the judging panel, they'd pass you right by."

The contestants move forward and turn once. My older sister looks lost and small in the towering forest of poised beauties. Some of the contestants know how to walk like models do on television, and they glide forward and then stop to stand like a photograph you might see in a magazine. Stacey Pratt arches her neck and looks at the crowd with self-assurance, like she knows she's a winner, like she has *winner* written all over her.

Granddaddy leans across the seat and whispers to me, "I think Melinda is by far the most beautiful. She outshines everybody. Don't you think?"

I don't know anymore what I think. I think the moon turned purple and fell out of the sky. That's what I think. I think the stars dropped from the universe and are clattering all over the roof above us sounding like rain. That's what I think. Everybody is smiling and acting normal, but nothing is normal. My older sister looks small and thin and overwhelmed.

"Now I would like to announce the third-place winner. . . ."

I am not listening anymore. This night belongs to somebody else. It isn't our night. We came here thinking it was going to be our night and suddenly we're outsiders, strangers looking in at something through glass, something we have no part of. We are only here to make the winner feel more important. Suddenly we're just a group of strangers standing on the sidelines.

After the ceremony, they serve refreshments: cider, sweet tea, cookies, and doughnuts. Melinda is hovering near the cider dispenser pretending to look at a flyer somebody was handing out earlier, advertising time-share condos in the Bahamas. I know time-share condos are about the last thing in the world my older sister is interested in, and sure enough, it happens. She bursts into tears. Mama leads her out the door and waves to Granddaddy and me to follow.

Stacey Pratt took the win. Right now she's getting photographed by the *Shenandoah Valley Newspaper* and the *Charlottesville Gazette*. There are about five cameras flashing on her. When you win something, everybody wants to take a big bite out of you and carry it away. They're chewing Stacey Pratt to bits, as far as I can see.

Granddaddy takes my hand and we push through the crowd. Quentin Duster cuts in front of us as we're going out the door. He knocks right into me, and his cider goes flying off down into the hay and mud on the ground in front of the pavilion. Typical Quentin. I roll my eyes and look away, not wanting to talk to anybody right now.

Granddaddy and I don't go on any of the rides. We even pass up the bumper cars and we walk right by the hypnotist tent, listening to the crowd inside swooning. We don't look at the scrubbed-up clean blue-ribbon Jersey cows. We don't go to see Quentin Duster's little brother's prizewinning black goat. All of us just stand in the rain under two umbrellas waiting for our ride. (The third umbrella got away from us back along the river where we were stuck, and I bet it's ripped to shreds by now.) Frank Bailey's brother-in-law is leaving early and he's going to give us a lift home.

As we stand here, Melinda is crying, leaning against Mama like a tree leans against a house in the wind. "Go figure," says Mama. "Stacey Pratt isn't even pretty."

"Confidence is everything," says Granddaddy. "If you're sure of yourself, everybody's snowed by your sureness. Just like Big Box Home and Hardware.

They come in with all this confidence and bunch of shiny junk, making them the winners right now, but they're the losers in my opinion. LOSERS," shouts Granddaddy.

"Granddaddy," says Mama, "if you raise your voice one more time, I'm going to haul off and swat you."

Mama puts her arm over Melinda's shoulder. "Honey," she says, "I know it's hard to lose. It's easier to win. But people don't realize that it's the ones who lose that really win in the end, because they have to build themselves back up, brick by brick. They have to put themselves back together after they lose. And *that* makes a person strong, Melinda. STRONG. And then when you run into big windstorms and terrible hurricanes, you're going to be so strong, *nothing* is going to pull you down. That's better than winning a beauty contest, isn't it, Granddaddy?"

"Honey, we know you're the prettiest. Who cares what a bunch of LOSERS think anyway?" says Granddaddy.

I look at my sister, Melinda, with tears running down her face, mud and rain all over her pink delicate skirt.

For once her curls have fallen out and her damp hair lies dark and sad on her shoulders. But it's her salmon-colored dyed shoes that tear right at my heart. They're all covered with water stains as she stands in the hay and mud right now. They're ruined, as far as I can see. In fact, suddenly Melinda and I have a lot in common. It seems as if we are both struggling in a world that hardly has room for us. Or if there is any room, it looks like it's going to have to be fought for.

When we get home and I'm lying in my bed, I notice the sky has cleared. The rain has finally stopped and everything is still and dark. I can hear the spring peepers in the swamp singing their hearts out, all those little unknown voices calling to someone, asking to be heard. Because we didn't win, there is a sadness covering me like one of my old wool blankets from my head to my toes. Even so, a feeling keeps surfacing in me, remembering how that audience clapped after Melinda read my poem. Even though she said it was her poem and they didn't know it was my poem, still it felt good to hear them clapping, knowing they had liked those words that I wrote, that they had listened to what was in my heart and they had liked it. I pull my curtains aside so I can see the black clean sky and I finally fall asleep, listening to all those spring peepers calling and calling and calling.

chapter 19

Come to find out in the morning, my whole world falls apart. Quentin Duster gets on the school bus with his little brother and Conrad isn't with them. At first it doesn't register. I feel confused, cloudy. Did Conrad get on ahead of Quentin? Did I miss something?

Quentin plunges down next to me with all manner of lunch boxes and book bags, plastic dinosaurs falling all over the floor and on the seat between us. Quentin's breathing heavy and fast. "I tried to tell you," he says to me. "I tried to tell you last night, but you just pushed on by, knocked the cider right out of my hand."

"Tried to tell me what?" I say.

"Conrad's going in the hospital today, getting his operation. It's serious. He could die. You could never

188

see him again and you didn't even say good-bye to him," says Quentin.

"I didn't know," I say. "Nobody told me."

"I tried to tell you," he says again.

I can't say much more about the bus ride. I can't say much more about anything. I don't see what we're passing. I don't hear what Quentin is saying to me. . . . Is he shouting? I thought I had more time, I am thinking. I didn't realize Conrad's operation would be so soon. I can't believe I didn't say good-bye to him. Tears are rolling down my cheeks and I try to keep my head turned so Quentin won't see. If Conrad dies, I'll die. But if he pulls through and his leg is back to normal, he won't need that old leg brace and then he'll play soccer again and then he'll be so popular, I won't be able to get near him. Then I'll be finished too. Either way I'll die.

I look at that mean old river, all fat and green and evil, winding along the road. Look how much trouble it caused us last night and now it's acting all nice and normal, trying to look like any old regular river when I know it's a menace.

First thing I do when I get to school, I put my head on my desk and I don't want to answer anybody.

Louise is pestering me. "Too bad your sister didn't win," she says.

"It was fixed judging. Granddaddy told me so," I say, lifting my head for a moment. Then I put my head back down. I figured out one afternoon during history class that if you drop the letter *I* from Louise's name, you get LOUSE. And she is a louse.

My teacher, Mrs. Duster, comes up to my desk. I know it's her 'cause I can smell the coconut hand cream, and when I open my eyes, I can see a little magnet taped to her right wrist. She's into magnets. She thinks putting magnets on her wrists helps her life in some way. It does something to her energy field, she told my mama, brings her happiness and peace. "Jessie Lou," she says now, "I really want you to redraw that self-portrait. Come time for the end-of-the-year dance, I want to hang all the graduates' S.P.s in the hall. I want you to redo it. I want you to rethink it. Okay?"

"Okay," I say. If I were to paint my self-portrait right now, I'd put a dark hollow in my interior as big as a black hole in outer space, full of nothing at all. Absolutely nothing.

When I open my eyes just a crack, I can see Conrad's chair looking about as vacant and empty as you can get. I know it sounds stupid, but it looks like a lonely chair, like a chair that's been ignored and overlooked for the whole school term, like a chair that's been battered and beaten but it still stands there with quiet self-assurance. It still comes back with a clever joke and an all-knowing sense of what's cool and what isn't.

Moon n' Stars is walking by Conrad's chair and it makes me uneasy the way she leans toward it. I want to go over to his chair and throw my arms over it and call out, "Leave it alone. It's *my* chair." Instead I sit here thinking about all the nice things Conrad's done in his lifetime. Like the day we took that trip to Monticello, Thomas Jefferson's mansion, way before I even really knew Conrad. Since Mama works, Granddaddy got to be the chaperone for the bus trip. But once we got to Monticello, Granddaddy wouldn't get off the bus 'cause he said Thomas Jefferson had a double standard. Wrote about freedom and justice for all and at the same time he was keeping slaves. "You go along with your class, Jessie Lou," he said to me. "I'm staying here on the bus. My job is bus proctor. I don't want to walk around and look at a bunch of lies."

So Granddaddy stayed on the bus the whole time and it was Conrad who kept coming back to the bus, bringing Granddaddy a bag of chips and a cup of coffee. Later he brought him a newspaper. Nobody asked Conrad to do those things. It's just part of who he is.

Another time, just this week, Quentin Duster got on a terrible jag on the computer at the library. He'd been playing Pac-Man for five hours straight and couldn't stop. He just couldn't. He was looking all washed away like a real live zombie, eyes glazed, throat parched, and still he wouldn't quit. So Conrad went over and pulled the plug on the computer, even though you're not supposed to. Put an end to it right then. Brought Quentin Duster back down to Earth. Nobody asked Conrad to do those things. It's just part of who he is.

Finally I lift my head up off my desk. I get up slowly and go over to the paper shelf. We're having art class and most people are working on the subject of abstract art. *Abstract Art: What is it?* our teacher has written on the chalkboard. Underneath that question there is a list of answers. Elizabeth Parnell wrote: 1) It's a mess of colors. Ryan Ferguson wrote: 2) It's ugly. Louise the Louse wrote: 3) It doesn't look like anything.

Everybody is trying their hand at abstract art, throwing colors around. Quentin Duster has more paint on his face than on his paper. I'm over here half looking out the window, half trying to get myself to start my new self-portrait. Finally I pull out a big huge sheet of blank paper and I lie down on it. I look up at the ceiling. If Conrad dies, I'll die too. I think about Conrad lying in the hospital on the edge of life and death and I didn't even say good-bye to him. Our discovery report crosses my mind too, and those T-shirts Tiny wants. Everything flies around in my mind like a bunch of worrying birds.

"Quentin," I say. "Get over here and draw an outline around my body, will you?" Quentin hears me, but he takes his sweet time. Then he hops over with a big blue messy paintbrush and paints a fat blue line all around my body while I'm lying here.

Then I get up off the paper. I don't know what else to do with my self-portrait. I don't feel like adding anything more to myself. I feel like I'm changing, that things are in turmoil inside me, that I don't want to put anything down on the portrait. There's just a big blue messy line around me to say that I am here and that I'm thinking about things. I write *Jessie Lou Ferguson* under the outline and I hang it up next to all the others. Then I tear down the other one I did before that said *STUPID. UGLY. SKINNY.* and I rip it up and throw it in the trash can next to the teacher's desk. She gives me a nod of approval.

Then Mrs. Duster's up at the front of the class, squeaking chalk on the chalkboard again. "One of our students, Conrad Smith, is in the hospital. I'm going to put his room number and address up here and I want y'all to write him a card or go visit him if you get a chance," she says. Teachers are very nice, but a lot of times they have no idea what's going on. She is talking to a brick wall and doesn't even know it. She hasn't even noticed in these eight months that Conrad isn't popular anymore. She hasn't noticed that nobody popular ever talks to him. She doesn't know that nobody in that class is going to send a card to Conrad.

Nobody is even going to give him a thought (except for me and Quentin).

However, the address she wrote on the chalkboard gives me a ray of hope. Right now I put it in my mind that Quentin and I are going in to see Conrad today after school, while he's still alive, before the operation, while he's still Conrad the kind, Conrad the caring, Conrad the unpopular.

chapter 20

Quentin still has a spot of blue paint on his nose and it seems to match the sky behind him as we walk down our dirt road after school. We are headed to the hollow where Granddaddy's car got stuck. We are hoping that they have pulled it out of the water and that it can be driven. Even if it is still soaking wet, but the motor is going, I know I can talk my granddaddy into taking us to visit Conrad. I know I can talk my granddaddy into anything. He loves me so much, he'd do anything I want. Like he always says, "I'd get you the moon, sweetheart, if my ladder went that high."

It's a pretty day, all sunny, and dandelions are blooming down in the soft lime-green grass. You can hear the roar of bees working in the apple blossoms. A big truck just drove up behind us and roared through going way too fast. Mama always says somebody ought to let the air out of the tires of the reckless drivers around here. The truck whizzes through, and a group of birds fly up in a swarm, and when the truck has passed, we see one of the birds has been hit. It's a plain little bird my granddaddy calls a barn swallow. It flutters and flaps and then lies at the edge of the road in the grass, not moving. My granddaddy knows a lot about birds. Before the shopping mall construction site came to town, he used to go bird-watching at dawn and I used to go with him.

"Poor little bird," I say, looking down. "It's only hurt."

"Looks dead to me," says Quentin.

"Well, you could go find a box and a small jar up at the old house for me and I'll take the little bird home to my granddaddy," I say.

Quentin looks all hippity hoppity and nervous, but finally he agrees to go up to the house, and he comes back with an old shoebox. And I mean old. It has a 1940s lady on the outside lid looking all fashionable. I put fresh green spring grass in the box and a little jar of water and then I lift up the little bird in my hands.

It's soft and warm and I can feel it quivering. I lay it down in the grass and it lies there in the box without moving. We did this once before with a baby bird that fell out of a nest. My granddaddy took care of the bird till it could fly. He called it Hasenpfeffer.

"Come on, let's get going," I say. "We'll take the little bird with us, but we have to be careful with it."

"Jessie Lou," says Quentin Duster, "I think you're half crazy."

"Guess that's better than all crazy," I say. Then we head off down the road looking for my grand-daddy's car.

We're just running along Creek Road passing a line of those big round bales of hay in the field next to us. There appears to be something or someone lying on top of one of the bales. Though I try to stop him, Quentin starts to call out something noisy. I put my hand over his mouth so he just makes a bunch of weird sounds, and then somebody rolls over and sits up, and Lord love us, as Mama says, it turns out to be Tiny Bailey.

Tiny drops down off the squashed bale. He's got a bunch of comic books rolled up under one arm and he looks all ruffled up and sleepy. He's got some hay in his hair. He gets up on the road and looks back at us. I just kind of stand there staring, not saying a word, like I'm trying to swallow one of Mama's burned cookies. Finally Quentin says, "Hey, Tiny, nice day! Didn't mean to wake y'all up."

Tiny looks down at the road and then he turns around to walk away. With his back to us, he calls out, "I need those shirts by the weekend, Duster. After that, it's too late." We don't have a chance to answer him 'cause by the time something comes to us, he's out of range, and besides, we don't exactly have an answer.

Quentin says, "He cuts classes. That's why he's a fifth-year senior. Sleeps all the time 'cause of his size."

"Quentin Duster," I say, "is there anything you don't have a lamebrain answer for?"

"Yeah, there is one thing," says Quentin, smiling and looking up at the sky.

Knowing we need to hurry, I let the subject drop. I carry that poor little barn swallow and that box carefully as I can. We run hard, about doing splits in the air, just flying. And as we run, birds in the field rise up around us in a great dark singing cloud.

"We have to get to Conrad," I shout out, "before he gets operated on. We just gotta run faster."

"Hey, why are you always bringing up Conrad, anyway? You're always going Conrad this and Conrad that. You don't *like* Conrad, do you?" says Quentin, looking over at me as we run along the road.

"I like him," I say, "but I don't *like* him."

"Good," says Quentin. "Don't gross me out by liking that idiot."

It turns out we do get a ride in Granddaddy's Chrysler Imperial. He is driving up the road and he stops the car, leans out the window, and says, "On land and sea, you can't put this baby down. What'd I tell you? She's a tank. Thirty years old and still going strong."

We get in the car and Granddaddy takes the shoebox with the bird in it and puts it on the front seat next to him and then he hits the pedal (wet as it is), and before you know it, we're sailing along the highway and then we're pulling into the hospital parking lot.

I knew Granddaddy would agree to take us to the hospital, but I know he won't go in. As soon as he parks the car, he looks over at us and says, "Y'all go on in now, sweetheart. I'll stay right here with this poor little bird and wait for you. Those doctors are all crazy in there. Whenever they operate, they leave half their instruments inside you by mistake. No thank you. I'll be right here when you come out."

Quentin and I head out toward the entrance of the hospital.

"It would have been a lot nicer if we could have brought Conrad a present. I should have gone in the bookstore and got him a book about Lewis and Clark," I say.

"What's he need something like that for if he's about to die? What do you need when you're on the edge of death?" says Quentin, following the white line painted along the edge of the asphalt parking lot. "Nothing. Absolutely nothing."

"Can't take it with you," I say, feeling like I'm going to cry. Granddaddy waves good-bye to us from the front seat of the Chrysler Imperial, and Quentin and I go into the double doors at the Winifred P. Culpepper Memorial Hospital.

I'm not all that different from Granddaddy. I don't like hospitals either. We get on the elevator with this person in a wheelchair who is all wrapped up from head to toe in white bandages, just his eyes left showing, like a mummy. Reminds me of the one in the computer game "The Quest of the Missing Mummy," where the mummy escapes and goes after everybody. There's a nurse pushing the mummy's wheelchair.

"Just checking — is that you in there, Conrad?" says Quentin.

It isn't Conrad. Thank goodness. But the nurse is mad at Quentin and she makes us get off the elevator one floor early and we have to go up the back stairs to the third floor. We get lost down a couple of hallways looking for room 348, Conrad Parker Smith's room. Finally we find a door decorated with two clothespin angels and a tie-dyed T-shirt that says *If your land's posted, don't hunt on mine.*

"That'll be it," says Quentin.

Right next to the door there's a cart full of supplies, stacks of hospital gowns and face masks for the surgeons. Somebody has left the cart alone for a second, and Quentin, who's as fast as a hummingbird, grabs a hospital gown and one of the masks and puts them on.

Then he opens Conrad's door with a sweep. "Conrad Parker Smith," he says, walking into the room, "it's time for that operation. I'm ready to begin. Gimme that leg."

Conrad goes green for a minute lying in his bed and his eyes look kind of crossed. It starts to look like he's going to faint. But then I get in the room and I grab the mask off Quentin and the color returns to poor old Conrad's face.

"How did you two turkeys get in here?" he says. "If you were headed for the funny farm, they brought you to the wrong place."

"What's that thing you're all hitched up to, Conrad?" says Quentin, walking around the room. "It's mean and ugly-looking, looks like a bomb's ready to go off or something."

"It's a monitor. I'm going in for a groundbreaking operation. You're not even supposed to be in here. I got a special doctor from Washington, D.C. I was selected to be the first one he tries his new technique on."

I gulp. "A new technique?" I say. I haven't said anything at all up until now 'cause I'm so upset to see

Conrad dressed in green hospital pajamas, lying there looking like he's about to die. I can see his old leg brace thrown on the table near the window, and I just feel like I am going to go to pieces if I say one word. So I just stand here like a sorry old beanpole.

"Yep," say Conrad, pointing to the leg brace. "Doctor says I'm not going to be needing that old thing anymore."

My heart sinks. If it can get any lower, it sinks yet again. In a split-second I am remembering all the good times we've had in these last few weeks. Like the time Conrad and I decided to pull his bicycle out of the river once and for all. We picked the day Quentin Duster had to go to a family reunion over in Liberty Furnace so he wasn't around. When Conrad and I got to the river's edge, we kind of waded out into the water, green branches hanging over us, my skirt dancing around me in the current. I could feel mud squeezing up between my toes and little minnows bumping against my knees. It was sweet being waist-deep in that river with Conrad Parker Smith. Right then, I could have floated away on my back all the way to Culpepper County.

When we got to the bicycle, Conrad looked over at me and said, "Leg brace is as light as a feather in this water." His face was about half shining.

We pulled and shoved and laughed and finally we got that bicycle back up on the shore. We even rode it home together, me in the front steering, Conrad on the back hanging on, both of us laughing and falling off and laughing and falling off again.

"Yep," says Conrad, "not going to need that old thing anymore. I think they're taking me in a matter of minutes. I'm going in to get some tests done for tomorrow 'cause it's a special operation."

"Special?" I say.

"I'm gonna be getting something pinned, either the tibia or the fibia in my leg," says Conrad.

"You mean pinned like a sewing project," says Quentin, "like an old dress or something?"

"Well, maybe stapled is a better word," says Conrad.

"Stapled?" says Quentin. "Like a geography project?"

"I don't know," says Conrad. "They put in some kind of pin or staple in there and then all you have to worry about is setting off alarms in airports."

"Setting off alarms in airports?" says Quentin.

"That's all. That's it," says Conrad. "Once the pin is in, you're up and running."

"Well, pin the tail on the donkey," says Quentin.

"What's that supposed to mean?" says Conrad.

"Gonna be able to play soccer again, Conrad?" I say real quietly.

Conrad looks down in a hoping kind of way and then he smiles. "Doctor says so." And my heart drops just like that bicycle slipping down into the dark river.

"Conrad," says Quentin, "you're not going to believe this, but out of the blue, we ran into 'The Engine' again."

"I think we woke him up," I say.

"I heard he needs sixteen hours of sleep a night. And if he doesn't get that, he has to pick it up during the day 'cause of his size," says Quentin. "People have seen him sleeping at the vocational cafeteria right up on the table in the middle of the day. That's what I heard."

"Is that so," says Conrad.

"'Cause of his size," says Quentin.

"Well, I heard once he slept for a whole week straight and his daddy had to drop him into a swimming pool in subzero weather to get him to wake up," says Conrad.

"Whoa," says Quentin, making like to wipe his brow.

"Conrad," I say, "your mama still want to get rid of those red T-shirts? Guess they really need them over there right away. Do you know where they are? I mean, since you're not gonna be home and all."

As soon as I say that, I feel kind of all alone and deep down blue. Then I look over at Conrad and I feel like dropping to the floor and begging him not to go and get himself all fixed up. I want to call out, "Conrad, don't do it. Keep things the way they are. Don't die and don't leave me and don't start playing soccer and getting popular again."

"Come on," says Quentin. "Where are those shirts? Exercise your memory, Conrad. Do some push-ups in your brain." (Ever since I told them what those T-shirts are for, I've been hoping Quentin can act like a sixth grader and keep a secret for once in his life, even though I know he's just a pesky half-baked nine-year-old.)

Conrad lies back on the pillow and closes his eyes real tight, trying to think where those boxes of shirts are. I can see he's going through his messy old wreck of a house in his mind. Conrad lives in a sea of craft projects. A house like that could take weeks to unsnarl.

"Maybe under a bed or in the living room over by the TV," says Conrad. "I'm not sure. You can go on in there and find them. House is open. But it's going to be a pain."

"Some things are worth it," I say, feeling all melty and teary-eyed, trying not to look directly at Conrad. I go and stand at the window. I can see the parking lot below and Conrad's mother just getting out of her car, probably coming back from the store down the street, picking up a few things for Conrad. I guess the truth is, I'd rather have Conrad popular again and lost to me forever than die. Dying is the worst of the choices. It doesn't matter if Conrad isn't going to be my friend anymore. All that matters is that he'll be alive and that others can enjoy him, if not myself.

Two nurses come into the room pushing a rolling hospital bed. The nurses are fast and quiet. "Have to say 'bye now," one of them says, smiling. They lift Conrad on to the rolling bed and they wheel him right out of the room headfirst. And the last thing I see of Conrad Parker Smith is his big toe sticking out from under the sheet that they've draped over him.

chapter 21

Call me crazy. Call me dumb. Call me foolish. I don't care. I have to find those T-shirts. If my granddaddy and the Bailey brothers need them, I gotta find them, and I'm not getting Quentin in on this or telling him any more about it because Quentin can only keep a secret for about twenty-four hours and then he might explode and tell everybody everything.

After we get back from Charlottesville and Granddaddy is putting the car in the garage, I walk off down the road like a little old ghost. I have my wagon with me, hoping to haul the boxes back.

The coyotes don't hang around by Conrad's. The houses are too crowded down there, but there are owls hooting and I still sense the wind all around me. I almost feel as light as a net curtain sailing down the road in the darkness, like being in a dark room on a windy summer night, curtains set loose like wings, blowing all over the place. The smell of lilacs is drifting across the road, and houses are glowing like jars of light in the distance or like fireflies over a field in August.

At Conrad's house the door is unlocked. Thank goodness. I guess Conrad's mother must think all those boxes and broken furniture and piles of fabric everywhere would scare away any robber. I just turn the doorknob and I enter Conrad's damp and crowded house.

A lot of the lights have been left on as if someone is coming back any second. In the living room the wide-screen TV is on. Coverage of the war in Iraq is playing to nobody at all in the dark, lonely room. The TV casts an eerie light in the living room, and that light falls into the hallway, making weird shadows on the wall. A fluorescent lamp is on over the sink in the kitchen, and I can see piles of clothespin angels everywhere, and there are all kinds of angels on shelves staring at you, glass ones and wooden ones and plastic ones.

The house looks and feels messier with Conrad and his mother not here. Houses are like that. They seem almost to disintegrate when the owners are gone, even for a day. Flowers wilt in vases. Food spoils on shelves. When I was here with Conrad and Quentin last week, the mess seemed less noticeable. It seemed acceptable, unimportant, even funny, when Conrad was here making all kinds of jokes about it, but now, without him here, I am astounded at the clutter and the chaos.

I go right into Conrad's room. I lean down now to look under his bed, searching for two cardboard boxes with a hundred and fifty T-shirts in them that all say *Best Things in Life Aren't Things.* All I see under the bed is a lineup of old shoes staring me in the face. There's also a beat-up teddy bear of Conrad's lying on its back, covered with dust, that looks like it's been there at least forever, judging from the cobwebs.

I never had a teddy bear when I was a little kid. I didn't care that much about my dolls either. Melinda had so many dolls and they were all dressed up in frills and lace and she never would let me play with them. I had instead these cookies I played with that I liked better. They were big gingerbread men that Mama made for all of us one Christmas. I saved mine. I had all fifteen of them and I made clothes for all of them and I put the clothes in the doll dresser Granddaddy made for me. All those gingerbread men had names. My favorite one was named Mr. Moon. He had a big round face and sometimes he slept on my pillow at night. I sewed him five different changes of clothes.

My mama used to say, "You're a strange breed, Jessie Lou." I guess she said that because Mr. Moon was my favorite toy and he was only a big old cookie. One day, after three years, I came home from school and all my gingerbread men were gone. Their clothes were folded up and put away in the doll dresser.

"Where's my Mr. Moon?" I called out soon as I came in the door, knowing something was wrong.

"Honey," said Mama, "the mice got into them this morning and I had to throw them away. We'll make a new batch today, okay?"

"What did you do with my Mr. Moon?" I said, running into my room.

We never did make a new batch of cookies, but by that time I was too old to be playing with toys anyway. But one day I decided Conrad looked a lot like

Mr. Moon. He had the same nice round cheerful face, and when I looked at him I got the same happy warm feeling.

I look next to Conrad's dresser now. There isn't much in it, 'cause all his clothes are on the floor. I look under his desk, in the closet. I look everywhere, but that box just doesn't seem to be anywhere at all. I feel kind of sad about Granddaddy and those old Bailey brothers hoping and waiting to get those T-shirts. I turn out the light in Conrad's room. I pass by the kitchen again. I open a few cupboards. I look under the table (even in the refrigerator!). I leave the light on over the sink the way it was when I came in. Then I stop for a minute in the living room, the TV dancing shadows on the furniture.

I am about to open the front door and leave when I see something red in the corner by the couch and if I tilt my head I can read the words *Best Things in Life* . . .

I throw myself on the couch and I pounce on those boxes like a cat from the bushes and I reach inside to feel all the folded piles of shirts lying in there. Yes. Yes, I got them. I pick up one of the boxes and I hold it tight against me. Tight as I can. I put that box outside on the steps, and then I go back to get the second one.

Now I need to get out of here as fast as possible. I pull open the front door, and as I'm slipping out, the wide-screen TV is still on. I can still see coverage of the war flickering into the dark room. In one corner of the screen a truck is burning. There are orange flames shooting up around it and all across the rest of the screen is nothing but blowing white sand.

chapter 22

This is the third day since I saw Conrad in the hospital and I haven't heard a thing. The silence is about killing me. The last two days have been long and lonely. Yesterday, Granddaddy had Fred Bailey over. They were sitting at the table in the kitchen organizing a rally and protest against Big Box Home and Hardware while Mama was grocery shopping up at Piggly Wiggly.

"We'll get out there with posters and we'll block the door. We'll lie down on the sidewalk. People will have to step on us to get in," said Fred Bailey.

"Well, we need to come at them from all angles — air, land, and sea," said Granddaddy. "We'll use brains and strategy."

"I'll get out my great-grandfather's Civil War uniform," said Fred Bailey. "I'll wear it at the protest, and

I'll hold up a sign that says, 'STONEWALL JACKSON WILL NOT BACK DOWN.'"

Then Granddaddy got mad and said he wasn't going to have anything to do with that bigot Stonewall Jackson.

I was waiting for news of Conrad. I was sitting there listening, hoping somebody would mention his name. But nobody ever did.

Two long, endless days have passed. Melinda has been pretty much holed up in her room playing her *Patsy Cline Revisited* CD over and over again. That afternoon when Granddaddy and Fred Bailey were arguing about the protest, I went upstairs. Melinda's door was shut. I sat on the top stair for a while, looking at the rose pattern on the wallpaper.

Then I did something very un-me-like. I tapped on the door and then I opened Melinda's door and I stood there. She was lying on her bed looking up at the ceiling, listening to that song "Crazy." She had the CD on replay and she was listening to it over and over again. She looked at me and didn't make an unpleasant face, so I went into her room and I sat down in a chair. She kept staring at the ceiling. I wanted to say something about how beauty wasn't all that important. I wanted to say that she was beautiful anyway, no matter what the judges said, but I couldn't figure out how to put it. So I just kind of sat there in the room with her for a while, listening to the music.

Yes, these few days have been long and lonesome — the longest two days I've ever experienced. Quentin's daddy got a job at Pool World and he brought home a stupid-looking snorkel set for Quentin. Quentin brought it down yesterday and he wore it running around the yard looking like an idiot space alien. "You're supposed to use those in a swimming pool underwater, Quentin," I told him. But he didn't listen to me.

A new Martha Nottingham Cake Mix came out two days ago with chocolate chips and coconut fudge and pecans. Mama and I made up a batch for Granddaddy's bowling night. And everything has been kind of slow, and no matter who I'm talking to, I feel kind of all alone. The shadows in the house at night seem extra dark. The clothes hanging on the line outside seem to be whipping around in the wind like they are crying and carrying on about something.

I have been drinking gallons of sweet tea, trying to decide about a lot of things, like what I'd do if Conrad dies and what I'd do if he doesn't die, and I've been working on those T-shirts, crossing things out and adding words. There's so many of them my arm feels tired.

It's after dinner on the third longest day of my life. We are watching TV. Melinda has come out of her room and she is in the La-Z-Boy recliner and I'm on the couch. The news starts and Granddaddy is just saying how TV is ninety-five percent advertising and ninety-five percent bull and no thank you and he is getting up and leaving the room.

Suddenly Conrad's face appears, covering the TV screen. The newscaster says, "And now in our Health Feature, we will be talking with a young man from the West Taluka Falls area who just underwent a successful operation with the famous Dr. Jerome Wildy! Dr. Wildy, how are you feeling right now?" says the newscaster.

"We're very excited," says Dr. Wildy. "This is the first operation I've done using this new pin I've developed and it was entirely successful. With a little physical therapy, the young man here will enjoy a complete return to normal activities fairly quickly. He's been using crutches for the first couple of days here at the hospital, but when he's ready, he can just throw those aside. That is the beauty of this new technique."

And then the camera switches to Conrad. "Well, Conrad Smith," says the newscaster, "how are you feeling?"

"Wonderful," says Conrad. "I've been walking all over the halls in the hospital. The nurses have practically had to tie me down."

"I understand you've got a sixth-grade graduation dance coming up that you're not going to miss this year. Am I right? And now that you're all fixed up nice, you can have your pick of any little girl you want to take. Am I right?"

"Hope so, it's about time," says Conrad, smiling, "and there are a lot of pretty girls in my class. It's almost going to be hard to choose." The newscaster laughs. Melinda laughs. Granddaddy laughs. But I cry. Deep down inside

I cry. The camera zooms out, and Dr. Jerome Wildy and Conrad with a small Day-Glo crutch under one arm are seen walking down the hospital hall together gesturing and talking.

"Nice little human interest story for a change," says Granddaddy, going into the kitchen to get himself another Snack Pack chocolate pudding. Then he calls out, "Isn't that a boy from your school, Jessie Lou?"

The newscaster goes on now to talk about other things, the upcoming air show and the opening day festivities planned for the end of the week, when the new shopping mall and Big Box Home and Hardware will be opening their doors.

Suddenly our phone is ringing. It is Louise the Louse. "Hi, Jessie Lou," she says. "Did you see Conrad on TV? Didn't he look handsome? I can't wait to see him. He's famous. He's been on TV. I'm going to get his autograph."

After I hang up the phone, it rings again. It's Elizabeth Parnell, the once-in-a-while-who-are-you friend I used to have. "Hello, Jessie Lou, good to talk to you. Have you been watching the news tonight? Did you see Rad on TV? Wasn't Rad funny?"

"Rad?" I say.

After I hang up the phone, it rings again. Sarah Jane Peabody, Tiffany B., Moon n' Stars Montgomery, and even Brice Buttonwood call here. Every piccolo player in the class rings my number. And the phone keeps going all evening. It rings and rings and rings. Practically half the people in our school call to say they saw Conrad and that they love him and that he is famous and isn't it a miracle and isn't Dr. Wildy wonderful? Didn't Conrad handle the publicity with ease? Wasn't it just too cool? Yes indeed, before Conrad even stepped one foot out of the Winifred P. Culpepper Memorial Hospital, his popularity was entirely restored and then some.

chapter 23

Three more days of even darker darkness. The sun barely shines. The clouds are mean and warlike. The river is indifferent, cold. The trees are strangers turning away from me. Of all the birds that are singing and carrying on for spring, it is the catbird I listen to. It sounds like a human baby crying in the treetops. But how would a human baby get way up there in the leaves and sky?

I skip school. I trick Granddaddy into thinking I am getting on the bus this morning and then I don't. I have never tricked my granddaddy before and it makes me feel even worse to do it.

"Okay, sweetheart," he says, "have a nice day at school." And he hands me my lunch bag with a special cheese-and-tomato sandwich that he made for me and the last peanut butter cookie in the house that I added to the bag myself, secretly. I usually have to hide a few of those cookies 'cause Granddaddy has a real bad sweet tooth and he'll gobble up any peanut butter cookies that get brought into the house. (Mama says Granddaddy's just plain devious when it comes to cookies.) Sometimes he even ferrets around and finds the hidden ones. But not this time. I can feel that cookie in the bottom of the bag, and it kind of makes me feel terrible too, knowing I'm keeping it from my poor old granddaddy.

I wave the bus on from the opposite side of the road. I duck behind the bushes so Granddaddy can't see me, and then I cut off down the hill with my lunch under my arm. I hate to do it to my granddaddy, but I can't face what I know is waiting for me at school.

Quentin Duster sees me and he has eyes as wide as two plates setting side by side on a shelf, watching me waving the bus on, knowing I'm skipping school. I can see him wriggling out of his seat trying to get the bus to stop, but it doesn't. It just keeps rolling on the way buses do, headed straight for school. Quentin is trapped, but I am free. Let him field all those questions. Let him witness all those turncoats turning yet again.

Maybe it isn't such a bad day outside, but inside me it is storming. Outside the sun keeps sailing in and out of those clouds, showering me with light and then showering me with shadows. I sit on a rock in a field of dandelions, letting bees buzz around me, watching the wind roll across the field, rippling it like a big green loose-weave rug.

My granddaddy says you have to bounce in this world. Just like a big beach ball. "You're going to get hurt sometimes," he says. "You're going to fail once in a while, but you got to bounce back like a big bouncy ball." If I were a ball right now, I'd roll away to the sea and I'd never come back.

I can still hear the newscaster on television saying, "Well, young man, looks like now you can invite any little girl you want to that dance."

And Conrad answers, "Hope so, it's about time, and there are a lot of pretty girls in my class. It's almost going to be hard to choose." I don't want to lose Conrad, but I know I already have. I can feel it. It's in the air.

It's in the birds singing. It's in the wind blowing. It's in the river rushing, still fat from the storm. It's in the dandelions, all yellow and dancing, thousands of them.

I've lost Conrad Parker Smith. I cry 'cause I'm alone and I know nobody can see me and crying is the only way to get rid of that horrible rock in my throat that is hurting so bad. I sob, thinking I'm all alone, but then I realize I'm not. I can see my sister, Melinda, walking through the field with a butterfly net and a notebook. When she gets within shouting distance, she calls out that she has the morning off and she's looking for milkweed pods and monarch butterflies for a paper she is writing for school.

Eighth graders call them "papers." Sixth graders call them "reports." Whatever they are, they're a whole lot of trouble, and I haven't even thought about our discovery report due at the end of the year. It hasn't even crossed my mind for days.

I kind of doubt Melinda will find any monarch butterflies at all since Granddaddy says they've gone scarce because of all the spraying of pesticides everywhere. "We have a lot of milkweed here, but we don't have the monarchs anymore," Granddaddy often says, slapping a book down on the table. "Used to see whole fields of them. Now you're lucky if you see a one."

Melinda walks toward me in the tall grass with her butterfly net and her eyes squinting under the changing sun. "Jessie Lou," she says, "are you crying?"

I say, "No, I am not crying." She sits down on the rock too, and we look at the field and the bees and the dandelions and the shadows of clouds coming and going. And then suddenly I start crying again. I can't help it. Then she starts crying too. We both sit here sobbing. I know why she is crying, but she doesn't know why I am crying, and that doesn't seem fair, me knowing and her not knowing. So I tell her. I don't mean to, but when something wants to pop out of me it just does and I never have been able to stop it. "I lost Conrad," I say. "And I love him to pieces. I lost him. He's looking forward to inviting any number of girls to the dance coming up. He won't need my friendship anymore."

Melinda looks right at me with her green eyes, so green as to mimic the fields all around us, her face so smooth as to be like one of those glass angels in Conrad's kitchen. "Jessie Lou," she says, "he isn't going to be the only boy you ever like. He may be the *first* boy, but there's going to be a whole lot more in your life coming up. I promise you that." She gives me a nice little smile, tilts her head, picks up my lunch bag, and says, "What y'all got in here anyway?"

We decide to split the sandwich. It tastes pretty good. Then I get out the peanut butter cookie and we make a real accurate line with Melinda's ruler that she has tucked in her notebook. We make the line right down the middle of that cookie and we break it in half to the absolute point of perfection. Yes indeed, Granddaddy would have eaten this cookie long ago, if I hadn't hidden it in the back of the kitchen cabinet under two saucers and a teacup.

chapter 24

Next day I go to school. I face the music. I think of myself as a ball. I bounce off the bus. I hop down the hall. It's Conrad's first day back at school, but I can't get near him. There are crowds of kids pushing around him trying to get his autograph. I can't imagine why — Conrad has the worst handwriting in the world. Girls are pushing and shoving in the hall trying to talk to him. Tomorrow night is the big sixth-grade dance and all the girls are talking about going with Conrad. In the girls' room they are drawing straws for who gets to ask him first.

Quentin is even pushing in the crowds by the front door trying to get Conrad's autograph. I nudge Quentin in the arm as I walk by. "Quentin Duster," I say, "what the heck are you doing?"

"I'm trying to get Conrad's autograph," he says. "Conrad's famous. Dr. Wildy might be asked to visit the president. I'm going to get that autograph. I'm only twenty-second in line."

"Quentin," I say, "Conrad isn't any different now than he was before he got on TV. He's still just plain old, stupid Conrad. What do you want his sloppy left-handed signature for anyway?"

I go into our classroom and I sit down at my desk. There isn't anybody in the room at all except for me and Mrs. Duster. She looks at me a long time like she's trying to read a sign that's too far away. I slouch at my desk and look down. She pulls a Weight Watchers frozen lunch out of her bag, preparing to take it to the refrigerator in the teachers' room next door. She arranges some papers on her desk and then she says, "Jessie Lou, aren't you going to add anything more to your self-portrait for tomorrow night? You're the only person up there who hasn't got anything at all to say about themselves."

I look away like I don't hear her, like I'm busy watching something invisible in the air. I am repeating to myself, nodding my head up and down in a knowing kind of way, *Popular people are not nice to unpopular people. It's just the way things are. Kids are fickle like the Cabanash River rising and falling. I've seen them be fickle over and over again.*

The bell rings and everybody scatters like a bunch of mud bugs when you turn over a rock. Everybody starts rushing toward their classrooms. Conrad comes through the door with Elizabeth Parnell, Moon n' Stars Montgomery, Sarah Jane Peabody, and Louise the Louse all draped around him. Hannah, Emily, and Tiffany B. are close behind. Jenny Bonners is beaming because she has his autograph, *CONRAD PARKER SMITH*, written with a Magic Marker in big letters on her arm all the way up to her elbow. Brice Buttonwood is standing next to him with his hand on Conrad's shoulder. Conrad is smiling, walking straight, looking happy, giving everybody all kinds of attention. He even waves to me from afar, the way a candidate waves to a potential voter he barely knows.

I feel like I'm going to faint. I feel all dizzy and I ask to go to the nurse's room. As I walk down the hall I try to bounce with each step. I bounce past the decorating crew working on the hall for the dance. They are hanging up red, white, and blue streamers.

"We're going with a patriotic theme this year, Jessie Lou," Paula T. calls out to me. "What do you think?"

"Looks real nice," I say.

I know how kids can turn on each other. I know how keeping on the right side of the crowd can be tricky and unpredictable. The tables have turned on me many a time. It isn't the first time. This time though, I say to myself, I'm going to bounce. And I do. I bounce like a ball down the hall. I bounce past the principal's office. I bounce right past the nurse's office and I bounce right out the door.

When I get out on the road, the sky is mixing around like water coming to a rolling boil. I'll probably make it home in time for lunch, though I feel too upset to eat one little bite. I think I'll just sit at the table while everybody else is wolfing down everything and I'll cut coupons out of the Piggly Wiggly flyer, helping Mama get ready for "Two for Tuesday," double coupon day. That's the only time Mama doesn't say, "Honey, you better start eating. You know a girl your size should be getting 1,200 to 1,500 calories per day. There's a fine line, Jessie Lou, between skinny and scrawny. You don't want to cross that line."

"I probably already have," I usually say. "Guess I crossed that line a year ago and didn't even give a hoot about it at the time and still don't."

As I'm running along, I try to make sense of everything. But nothing seems to make sense. I just found out as I was leaving school what all those white envelopes were that Brice Buttonwood was handing out that day on the bus. Brice was selecting popular kids to go up to Buttonwood's Bowl-a-rama II during opening day celebration. They're gonna be putting on a Lewis and Clark discovery skit with costumes and props and everything. Today Conrad was asked to be Clark. Brice will be Lewis, and the wonderful discovery they'll be making will be the new Bowl-a-rama. How can Conrad play Clark when he's been Lewis for all these weeks? It just makes me feel like losing it in the road.

I pass the old meandering Cabanash River, the river that knows everything and says nothing. I pass the spot where Conrad pushed his bike in a long time ago — or at least that's what it feels like. Then I reach down and pick up a handful of gravel and throw it up high till it falls into the river, making a shower of little stones. It seems like where things fall is just up to gravity and luck, with no sense to it at all. I sit down on the edge of the bank and lie back and look at the sky.

When I finally get home, I don't even say boo to anybody. I just take a peek at the little barn swallow lying in the grass in the box in the hallway. Granddaddy's got birdseed and bread crumbs in there for it. I sit and hold the box for a while like to rock that bird to sleep. Then I just go up to my room to my desk and get out my big black Magic Marker and a pile of T-shirts. I've done fifty shirts already. (Granddaddy's done ten.) Just like Quentin once did, I cross off the words *Aren't Things* and I write in *Are Tulips*. So the T-shirts read, *Best Things in Life Are Tulips. Shop Bailey's Hardware.*

chapter 25

"Boredom is for people who don't have any imagination, honey. Life is too short to waste it being bored," shouts Mama, whizzing around my feet with the noisy nozzle of a vacuum cleaner. I am sitting at the kitchen table poking a bunch of cherry tomatoes with a chopstick, ruining them all. Somebody has left their Chinese fortune from a cookie on the table. It says, *Wise is the frog that hops away.*

I'm so glad today is Saturday. I won't have to witness Rad and Moon n' Stars and Elizabeth Parnell and Louise the Louse and all the others. I have all kinds of time on my hands. It isn't exactly boredom. It's just that I used to knock around with Conrad and Quentin, but now I don't. I poke another cherry tomato.

Granddaddy comes into the kitchen wearing his

fishing jacket, carrying a pair of binoculars, a camera, and his fishing hat. "Where are you off to, Mr. Ferguson?" says Mama, sucking up a stray sock with the vacuum cleaner by mistake. It gets caught on the end of her nozzle and makes a terrific racket, like something begging not to die. Granddaddy pulls the sock off the nozzle and takes his foot and clicks the vacuum cleaner off, bringing the room to a kind of startling silence.

"I'm going fishing, but on my way I'm going to stop over at the shopping mall to see the final results. They're opening up tomorrow. There's going to be all kinds of enticements on a Sunday morning to get people away from going to church, to go on down there and buy and buy and buy. Never mind what it is, just buy."

"There's going to be a real nice air show," says Mama. "Some man from Richmond is going to be shot out of a cannon. There's going to be all kinds of stunt airplane acts, planes going upside down and the like. Jack Duster told me another fella is going to skydive out of a helicopter and he's going to land in one of the pools from Pool World. There's a lot of skill involved in those stunts," says Mama, punching on the vacuum cleaner again, ending the conversation with a roar.

"You want to go, Jessie Lou?" shouts Granddaddy, putting his arm around me. 'Course I do. All I have to do today is poke cherry tomatoes with a chopstick. Can't get much worse than that.

When Mama said the air show was tomorrow, it kind of jolted me 'cause I haven't finished all those T-shirts. It tears my heart out to think Conrad will be going over to the new Buttonwood's Bowl-a-rama to be Clark of all people, so those shirts are up to me. I'm on my own now. I lay my head back against the car seat and I close my eyes and I don't open them till we are there.

At the shopping mall there is already all sorts of hoopla going on. They are pumping up an enormous air balloon on site in the shape of a huge Big Box Home and Hardware truck. It lies there with its big blue lettering getting fatter and fatter as the air is pumped into it. It is so big that it takes up a huge portion of the parking lot. There are all kinds of people standing in a big circle around it, looking at it with awe, admiring it like it is some kind of enormous circus animal lying on its side getting plumper and plumper.

We drive up to the edge of the parking lot. Moon n' Stars's mama is on the corner, wearing her big fat Earth Day globe costume, holding a sign that says SAVE THE EARTH. I blush and I don't want to get out of the car, but Granddaddy doesn't pay me any mind. He parks the car and opens the trunk. He gets out two fishing poles, a couple of fishing baskets, and two pairs of tall rubber waders. He hands me a pair and a pole. Then he gets out a big sign that says, WE SMELL SOMETHING FISHY. BIG FISH GO HOME.

"Keep it under your hat, sweetheart," Granddaddy says. "I mean where your mama is concerned."

Well, I don't really want to do it, but I get out of the car and I take the sign. Then Fred and Frank Bailey show up on their moped in fishing outfits too. Their signs say, SHOP AT FRED AND FRANK BAILEY'S FOR YOUR FISHING SUPPLIES.

"We're going with a fishing theme, Jessie Lou, figuring that's Bailey's strong point. We're hoping Big Box Home and Hardware won't be carrying fishing gear," says Granddaddy, putting on his waist-high waders.

Looks like this stuff has been planned behind Mama's back and somehow I got roped into it. I stand here on the hot sidewalk holding the big sign that's like a sail in the wind, pulling me one way and then pulling me the other. Moon n' Stars's mother walks toward us. I can see sweat on her forehead. It must be roasting inside that globe outfit. I want to ask her if Moon n' Stars got invited to the dance tonight by Conrad Smith, but as she walks closer, I decide against it.

We're all here now in our tall rubber waders, with our poles and our signs. We walk up and down the sidewalk. As we stand here, old-fashioned biplanes on flat trailer beds are brought in around us. Bleachers and platforms for speakers are being unloaded from several semi trucks. The Big Box Home and Hardware balloon truck grows bigger and bigger. More and more people bring in more and more equipment, speakers, microphones, more airplanes. Pool World is here setting up the giant outdoor aboveground pool. Trucks carrying lines of Porta Potties drive by us.

We walk back and forth on the sidewalk. Nobody pays any attention to us. Nobody honks at us. Nobody shakes their fists at us. Nobody seems to even notice us at all. We walk back and forth for two hours. I'm getting a sunburn and Moon n' Stars's mama is practically fainting from the heat inside her outfit, so finally we decide to go on home.

As we are walking back to our car, we pass the front of the shopping mall. There's a big gold abstract sculpture standing near the double doors. Just put in place this weekend. I know it is abstract 'cause of our lesson at school. Mrs. Duster explained that abstract art is something that doesn't look like anything. The statue doesn't appear to be anything at all, just a bunch of shiny gold metal pieces looping in and out of each other, looking important and baffling and stupid all at once.

"That's abstract art, Granddaddy," I say. "Learned all about it in school."

"Maybe so," says Granddaddy, handing me the binoculars, "but look over there on top of it. There's a bunch of something flying around and sitting all over that statue. What do you think they are?"

"Birds, Granddaddy," I say.

"Yeah, they are birds," says Granddaddy. "Statues

make great bird perches. But what kind of birds are they?"

"I don't know, Granddaddy," I say, looking through the binoculars. "They're black and white and brown."

"That's right, Jessie Lou. What did I tell you? What did I tell you?" says Granddaddy. "They aren't supposed to be in this region at all, but by golly, there they are. Those are magpies, Jessie Lou. Just a bunch of magpies."

chapter 26

By the time we get home, it is late afternoon. Mama has vacuumed the whole house, giving everything a kind of glow. Windows are open, and the smell of lilacs blows through the screens. The house is the kind of magazine-photograph clean that normally would make me feel special and happy, but today is not a normal day. I'm guessing Conrad has already picked a girl and asked her to the dance. They're both probably getting all dressed up right now.

"Catch anything?" says Mama as we walk into the beautiful, clean kitchen that makes you feel washed and fresh just stepping through the door.

"Nope," says Granddaddy, looking over at me with that sheepish, sorry look he gets when he's been ranting too much and he knows it. "Didn't get anything at all except a big headache."

I go on off to my room. Nothing left of the afternoon but to watch it fade away from my window upstairs. Nothing left but to watch it turn rosy red on the horizon and disappear. There is a lot going on this weekend. I know the sixth-grade graduation dance is being made ready. I can just feel the festivities being prepared. The air feels electric and charged like it's singing a song I can't hear, a song normal ears can't detect. I'm on the outside of those festivities, not a part of them. It always feels funny to miss a big event like that, like looking at a frame on the wall with no picture in it.

I sit at my desk and I write out two poems quickly. Both of them are stupid. I rip them up into confetti bits and let them fall out of my hand like snow. There's a stray piece of paper on my desk and I turn it over and it's that envelope I found in the old house. Just says *To Vera Bailey.* Is that the name of the person who lived in the old house?

I feel a double shiver of loneliness. I think about

calling Quentin Duster but then I change my mind. I open my window and watch the sunset. Best thing about my room. I've got a window onto the sunset just about every night.

I can hear a marching band in the distance, the drums sounding like a dark heartbeat inside me. The sound of the drums makes me remember happier times, like when we hosted the All-State here in West Taluka. I figure everything is going to change now. Conrad isn't going to need me to sit with him on the curb during any parades. He isn't going to need me to think of getting a triple chocolate Mister Softee cone just at the right moment. He isn't going to need my friendship at all anymore, now that he can have his pick of anybody he wants, now that his popularity has doubled or tripled and keeps on growing just like that dreadful enchanted porridge that pours into the streets and floods the town in that Grimm fairy tale.

I look out my window and I can see the lights across the valley opening up like little buds bursting into bloom in the new darkness. I hear that marching band in the distance again, and I know going back to school

I'll be marching straight into "the worst-case scenario," as Mrs. Duster says. Whenever some kid in our class is scared to do something, she'll go, "Let's talk it over. What's the worst-case scenario?"

I don't even think I can go back to that school ever again. I know I can't. I feel like I might break into a thousand pieces, like one of Granddaddy's jigsaw puzzles, like the time he dropped President Woodrow Wilson in a thousand pieces on the floor after spending a whole week putting him together.

I guess if I quit school, I would miss Mrs. Duster's comforting voice. Maybe I could go back if I had a bunch of her magnets taped to my arms. Mrs. Duster even sleeps on a mattress with magnets in it. Maybe she could tell me how I could get one of those mattresses that pull all the sadness out of you magnetically while you sleep.

I go over to my mirror and look in. I can see I have a pretty bad sunburn on my face. There's a pair of scissors lying on the dresser. I pick them up and I'm about to start hacking off my hair again when Mama calls up the stairs, "Jessie Lou, there's a boy on the porch with a big bag of candy for you."

"What'd you say, Mama?" I call back.

"Jessie Lou, come on down, honey. There's a boy on the porch wearing a fancy jacket with a bag of candy for you."

"For me?" I say.

"That's what I said, honey," says Mama.

"There must be some mistake," I call back. "You must have got it wrong." I am standing at the top of the stairs and then a shadow moves across the porch downstairs and goes to the screen door below and stands there looking in. The porch light is behind whoever it is, so I can't make out any features. Whoever it is, is wearing a white jacket slightly on the too-big side. And that person is wearing a little bow tie and holding a big bag of candy. And when that person turns his head a little so that the light falls across half his face, I can see then that person has a Mr. Moon smile and I close my eyes to keep from going dizzy.

"Jessie Lou, come downstairs. It's Conrad Parker Smith, honey, wants to invite you to the sixth-grade graduation dance."

"Me?" I say. I open my eyes and then I close them again because my heart is going down to my stomach and then back up to my throat just like an elevator making a fast run — first floor, fifth floor, first floor, fifth floor. I take a breath and then I open my eyes again and I look down at myself.

Me? I'm wearing worn-out jeans and a faded plaid shirt and a pair of black high-top sneakers, the kind boys wear. My face is all sunburned. Me? Suddenly, I don't want Conrad to see me. I don't want anybody to see me the way I look right now and then I say, "Uh, I don't have anything to wear. I can't go. Don't you have to wear pretty dresses to those kind of dances?"

Melinda is standing in the upstairs hall now. A moment ago she had been lying on her back in her room, looking up at her ceiling the way she has been recently. But then I saw her moving out of the corner of my eyes. I could see her walking toward the hall. She leans now against the door near me. She says, "Jessie Lou, you gotta go to the dance. I had so much fun two years ago when I went to that sixth-grade thing. You *have* to go."

"But I can't, I don't have anything to wear."

"Jessie Lou," she says, "I think I can loan you a dress. She'll be right there in about ten minutes, Conrad," she calls down the stairs. "Isn't that just like a boy to wait till the last two seconds to ask you to a dance? Don't give you but a minute to get ready, do they?" Melinda goes over to her closet and pulls out a pale purple-colored layered fluffy dancing dress with hundreds of little buttons up the back. It's a dress a princess or a queen might wear, a dress so soft and light as to be made of dragonfly wings, a dress you barely felt like you could touch, never mind wear.

Before I have a chance to say no, Melinda has me all buttoned up and inside that dress, looking down at it and around at it. A dress like that just makes you feel like turning in circles. Then she puts pink lipstick on my lips and a barrette in my hair, pulling what bangs I have off to one side. "That sunburn gives you color, Jessie Lou. Now the shoes are a problem 'cause we don't wear the same size," Melinda says.

"My only good pair are in Granddaddy's car and it's over in the repair shop getting its spark plugs changed," I say. In fact, all I have to wear for shoes are my black high-top sneakers, but I figure this fluffy dress is long enough to cover them up most of the time. Anyway, I don't have any choice — I *have* to wear them. It's better than going barefoot.

When I get downstairs, my mama clasps her hands together and says, "Oh, Jessie Lou, don't you look pretty. Turn around for me, honey, so I can see your hemline." Mama and Melinda are awful concerned about straight hemlines. Me, I don't think it's the end of the world if your hem hangs crooked. As I turn, my mama sees the black high-topped sneakers underneath my dress. She throws her arms around me and hugs me and says, "Oh, you're a rare breed, Jessie Lou. You're just my upside-down fairy princess. Got a style all your own. Got a style all your own."

Conrad's mama is waiting in the car in the driveway. As we leave the porch, Conrad hands me the big brown bag of candy, saying, "Here's some loot in case we get hungry." I take it, but I'm still feeling stiff and shy and stupid. I can't believe Conrad just gave me a whole big bag of candy and I didn't even have to fight for it.

We open the car door, and Conrad's mother gives me a corsage that she put together with a clothespin angel and a purple rhododendron. It matches my dress perfectly and I pin it on my shoulder.

Conrad and I sit in the backseat, and his mama starts up the motor, and Conrad says, "The school, Jeeves," pretending his mama is a chauffeur and that kind of breaks the ice and I laugh. Then Conrad's mama laughs and Conrad laughs and pretty soon everything's all normal — we're just a car full of laughing people backing out of a driveway.

Granddaddy's up on the porch now, waving to us as we drive off. He looks kind of sad and full of worry. He's not used to seeing me all dressed up, I guess. He keeps waving and waving like he's saying good-bye to me forever, like he's never going to see me again.

"Faster, Jeeves," says Conrad, falling back against the seat. The fields rolling by out the window make me think of my abandoned house and the old barnstormer airplane and the envelope *To Vera Bailey*. I have been dying to tell Conrad how I snuck into his house and got the T-shirts, how Granddaddy and I've been crossing out *Things* and putting in *Tulips*. I want to talk to him but the words just won't budge in my throat. Feels like even if I had a crowbar working away in there it wouldn't do me any good.

When we get to the school, kids' parents are pulling up in all kinds of cars. My used-to-be-friend Elizabeth Parnell and Sarah Jane Peabody have invited Josh Jameway and Michael Malten and the four of them have rented a stretch limo. It isn't the first time Elizabeth P. has ridden in a stretch limo. Her parents rented one for her last year when Elizabeth had to get a tooth pulled at the dentist. They rented the limo so she could watch her favorite video on the way there and back just to cheer her up. The one her parents have rented this time is a big long white limo and it's pulled up at the curb and kids are clustered around it acting like it's the coolest thing they ever saw and Sarah Jane and Elizabeth are getting star treatment as they step out in their party dresses.

As soon as we pull up, the stretch limo seems to shrink in size. It isn't all that long. It isn't all that cool. Conrad is way cooler. He's been on TV. He's famous. Maybe his famous doctor is going to take him with him on a tour. Hurry. Quick. Get his autograph. Grab him. Everybody is in a big circle around us, asking all kinds of dumb questions. Conrad just pushes his way through the crowd, smiling.

When we get into the school, things kind of settle down. The decorations are so beautiful — all red, white, and blue, so patriotic as to bring tears to your eyes. Even the principal's office seems to glow with streamers and flags. All down the hall are the huge self-portraits of all the sixth graders graduating, going on to junior high next year. A big banner across the top says, OUR SIXTH GRADE GRADUATING CLASS. WE LOVE YOU ALL. I try to look away when we pass mine. Mine has nothing on it, just a big blue line around the outside. Nothing else, just an empty white space inside.

If the halls dazzled me, the gym itself takes my breath away. It doesn't even look like a gym. There are tables with candles lit and flowers in big jars of water and there are streamers hanging from the ceiling and red, white, and blue balloons are tied everywhere. Music is playing in the darkness and there is a refreshment table lit by candlelight. Parents and teachers are sitting along the side, dressed up too. Everything feels like a dream. I stand here letting the warm darkness blow around me in the center of the gym, letting my dress billow out as I turn in a circle.

Conrad is headed for the refreshment table, and I take it in mind to do something. I slip out through the crowds of kids and I find myself a big Magic Marker in a desk and I go over to my self-portrait and I give myself two eyes, a nose, and a big old smile. And then I write all around the border, *HAPPY. HAPPY. HAPPY. HAPPY. HAPPY.*

When I get back to the gym there's a slow dance playing, and Conrad is sort of standing there, and suddenly we start dancing a kind of made-up waltz. We're faking big-time 'cause neither of us really knows how to dance and we're laughing about it. In fact we're roaring out of control, stepping all over everybody's feet. Then we start getting goofy and doing a sort of galloping step, horsing across the gym. Finally we stop over by the far wall and we get out the bag of candy and divvy up a bunch of M&M's and a Snickers bar.

Later when the music gets real loud and fast and you can't hear yourself think and we're all dancing in a big swarm, everybody looking like idiots waving their arms around, I shout to Conrad, "I got the T-shirts. I went to your house. I got 'em."

"You did?" says Conrad.

"Yes, I did," I say.

"I'm glad, Jessie Lou," Conrad shouts back. "It was the first thing I thought about when I woke up from my operation."

The rest of the evening is kind of a blur. For some of the dances Conrad stands along the back wall of the gym with all the other sixth-grade boys talking about shows they saw on TV. Other dances we aren't in the gym at all, we're running around in the empty cafeteria and down the long halls, enjoying the fun of running free all over the school at night. Later, when I'm dancing one slow dance with Conrad, my rhododendron corsage loses its petals. They fall all around me as we're dancing, leaving me with a clothespin angel with a big safety pin on the front of her dress, sitting on my shoulder. But I'm proud of that clothespin angel. Gonna keep it forever, hang it on my wall in my room, look at it every single morning soon as I wake up.

I have to say that during the whole night, Conrad's popularity is astounding. He can do no wrong, even when we're dancing and we step on other people's toes or on a long trailing skirt passing through. Everybody just makes jokes and laughs, nudging Conrad with their elbows or slapping him on the back. People wave to us when we go over to get cider. They call out, "Hey, Conrad, how's it going?"

Quentin Duster was banned from attending the dance since he's only a fourth grader, but he has weaseled his way into working at the refreshment table with a couple of the unsuspecting teachers, so he has a chance to take a few potshots at me and Conrad. But I don't care. I don't care about anything because when Conrad and I are dancing, I might as well be in the air show myself, skydiving through the darkness.

Funny thing has been happening when I am with Conrad tonight. Seems like some of his popularity has been rubbing off on me, and in a way, I feel like I am popular too. Everybody sure is being nice to me. I don't know how I look on the outside, but I'd like to say that I feel pretty on the inside, and Granddaddy always told me that's all that really matters.

chapter 27

I wake up the next morning to fireworks, loud explosions big as cannons going off during the Civil War. I can also hear a brass band playing, *Oh what a beautiful morning, oh what a beautiful day* over and over again. It comes in on the wind and it sounds halfway out of tune. I get up quickly and I get dressed quickly and I hurry downstairs. I know Conrad will be over at Buttonwood's Bowl-a-rama being in the popular Lewis-and-Clark skit, but I have to get these T-shirts to the Bailey brothers. I'm not going to the air show and opening day celebration. I'd boycott that anyway, even if these shirts were already delivered.

Mama meets me at the bottom of the stairs. "Going to church with me and Granddaddy and Melinda?" she says. "Better hurry, we're all ready."

I rub my forehead. "Graduation dance gave me a headache, I got to lie down."

"Sure wish you'd go with us, Jessie Lou," says Granddaddy, making sign language at me while Mama's not looking. He winks and nods his head and then he says, "Everybody should go to church this morning and pray, 'cause this is a dark day as far as I can tell."

"With your sense of drama, Mr. Ferguson, you should have gone into the acting field. You missed your calling," says Mama, giving Granddaddy a big kiss on his cheek. "Well, I suppose it's too late now, nobody would want to look at an old geezer like you onstage. Better get your reading glasses or you'll be bugging me through the whole service. 'Which Psalm are we on? What page are we on?'"

"Well, I'll tell you something," says Granddaddy. "Every time that minister tells us what Psalm we're on or what song we're gonna sing, he mumbles. Throws the whole vestry into a complete tailspin. And I hope we have a full house today. I hope all those fools that call themselves Christians aren't over at that shopping mall celebration."

"The world is changing and growing, Granddaddy. You better get with the beat. Wake up and smell the coffee," says Mama.

"I'm sniffing," says Granddaddy, "and all I smell is skunk."

Granddaddy opens the door and moves aside. Melinda and Mama go out and down the steps toward the garage, carrying matching white patent-leather purses.

As soon as they're gone, I click into action, get on my sweater, get my sneakers tied. In a matter of seconds I'm in the yard and flying like a low hovercraft two or three inches above the grass, speeding along, pulling my red wagon behind me.

When I get down on the path I hear voices in the air and I turn around. Lo and behold, as Mama says, Conrad and Quentin are running along the path making jokes just like old times.

"Thought you'd be up at Buttonwood's being Clark," I say.

"Nah," says Conrad. "It would be impossible for me to play Clark. I'm Lewis. I'm Lewis down to my bones." He smiles. And that's all we say about it. And I have no idea how Brice Buttonwood's Lewis-and-Clark skit will go without a Clark, and I guess I don't even care.

We can hear fireworks now going off in the distance. Boom. Boom. Boom. A thunderstorm? A war? No, just Big Box Home and Hardware taking over. *Oh, what a beautiful morning, oh, what a beautiful day.* Boom. Boom.

"By the way, you took your sweet time getting here, Jessie Lou," says Quentin. "And I have to tell you, boy, you two looked like a pair of donkeys dancing in the gym last night. Tried to say I didn't know you. Anyhow I can dance better than you, Conrad. I can do the real waltz. I could have danced with you, Jessie Lou, better than he does. No offense, but Conrad, you're rusty. You're out of practice."

Conrad smiles.

"I'm sorry I was slow getting here, but I had to wait till Mama went to church. My granddaddy wanted me to hush about all this," I say.

"You have my deepest sympathy," says Conrad, nudging Quentin. Then the two of them start laughing and they take off down the old logging road through the pine woods to the secret hidden field.

It is quiet down in the woods. The ground beneath us is thick with a soft bed of pine needles muffling our steps. Sun makes lacy patterns on the ferns, lacy patterns on our faces when we walk under an open shaft in the trees above. Then you can look up and see the blue sky. You can catch glimpses of the air show. Right now a big plane is flying across the sky dragging a banner that says, SHOP BIG BOX HOME AND HARDWARE. WE'VE GOT EVERYTHING YOU NEED.

We get to a larger clearing and we sit on a rock, the three of us. Looking up at the sky again, we see a helicopter working its way over us, and then we can see a little black dot dropping through the air.

"This is a big day for my daddy," says Quentin. "He's supervising an exhibition over there. You know a stuntman from L.A. is going to jump out of a helicopter and land in one of the pools from Pool World. That might be him right now. Hope he makes it. If he doesn't, my daddy will lose his job for sure."

We can hear more music now and more fireworks.

"What a waste, setting off fireworks in the middle of the day," says Quentin.

We head on down now farther into the woods, birds

fluttering across the path, chipmunks racing up trees, spiderwebs so complicated and perfect hanging half in shadows. We get to the edge of the field and we look out into the bright sunlight.

The beautiful little old barnstormer plane is sitting in the middle of the field. It is all cleaned up and the wings are on it again. It just takes my breath away. It's so shiny and silver. The last time we saw those enormous wide, stretching wings they were up in the rafters in the barn. Even then, their size was frightening. Now they are awe-inspiring, stretching out like arms big enough to hold the whole world. It moves my heart to see it, makes my heart fly just to look at it.

Soon enough we see Fred and Frank Bailey coming out of the opposite woods. Both of them are wearing old-fashioned flying goggles and old close-fitting canvas flying hats with chin straps that remind me of swimming pool caps. They both have on worn-out leather pilot jackets and they look exactly alike. There's no way I could tell you Fred from Frank.

As soon as we see them, we all blast out into the field with the boxes of red T-shirts, everything all windblown and full of sunlight. We come rushing up real close and stand with them next to the plane outside the little cockpit.

"We haven't done an air show in years," says the one I think is Fred, putting on his dog-eared flying gloves and then rubbing his hands together. "Used to be able to turn a baby like this upside down at low altitude."

"Yes, sir, you tell your mama thank you," says Frank, pulling the shirts out of the boxes. "We'll stuff them on the floor here. Boxes are too bulky to take with us. Can I ask you to put them on the porch for us up at my aunt's old place on your way home?"

"Whose old place?" I say.

"My old aunt Vera Bailey. It's her house and this was her plane. Always kept it in the barn."

"Oh," I say.

"Well, she was one of the *Ninety-Nines*," Fred says. "First group of women pilots in our country. There were ninety-nine of them."

"Oh," I say again.

"Something to be proud of. They couldn't keep her out of the sky. She just had to be up there. Didn't she, Frank?"

"Uh-huh," says Frank. "Guess we're a flying family."

"We like racing too," says Fred, raising his eyebrows. "Stand way back now when we take off and keep your fingers crossed. And if you like tulips, stop over at the store when you get a chance. They're one of our specialties."

Then Fred and Frank Bailey look up at the sky both at the same time, and they button up the straps to their flying caps at the same time, and pull down their goggles at the same time. Then, even though they're in their eighties, they look like a couple of twin babies sitting in their baby buggy, matching exactly.

Conrad and Quentin and I run to the edge of the field and stand there. I think Frank's the pilot but I'm not sure. According to Mama, he's the speed demon. Mama says, "That one throws care to the wind."

Frank Bailey gets comfortable behind the little steering wheel and his brother works himself into the seat behind him. Frank gives me a big cheerful wave and he turns on the engine and we hear the deafening roar. There are long white plumes of smoke coming out of the back, a smoky white peacock plume, a snow goose displaying its feathers. Then Vera Bailey's plane starts to move and it begins circling the field on its wheels. Around the field the plane bumps. Around and around. Bigger and bigger circles. And suddenly in a great roar, the plane rushes forward and it starts to lift up, up, up, off the ground. Up, up, up above the field. A little higher. Above the trees. A little higher. Around and around above the hill. Its thunder filling the air. Into the sky. Into the sky. Little old 1930s plane has made it. It's up in the sky.

Then it circles away over by the shopping mall celebration. It makes a turn over the crowd, and we see the T-shirts like so many little red flowers falling out of the sky, all of them saying, *BEST THINGS IN LIFE ARE TULIPS. BEST THINGS IN LIFE ARE TULIPS. BEST THINGS IN LIFE ARE TULIPS.*

Seeing those T-shirts, we run out into the field, calling out, "Hurrah!! Good luck to you. Good luck to you." We are running and running and then I drop to my back and lie there in the tall grass, looking up at the sky at the little barnstormer working its way around the air show and the Big Box Home and Hardware celebration.

Quentin and Conrad throw themselves down next to me. They are still screaming and shouting, "Good luck to you! Good luck and godspeed!" and then they roll over toward me and Conrad kisses my cheek and Quentin kisses my forehead.

"Get out of here," I say to both of them, swatting the air, and they take off, the two of them, laughing and calling and waving their arms toward the plane.

I can't see Vera Bailey's plane for a moment 'cause it dipped behind a cloud, but I can still feel Conrad's kiss on my cheek. I am lying in the field in the green Virginia grass, the sky a soft, breathing blue. Here I am a sheep-shorn scrawny somebody's little sister, and Conrad Parker Smith kissed me. He kissed me and the whole world is sweet and warm and full of soft Virginia wind. Conrad's kiss feels like a little butterfly fluttering against my cheek and then that little butterfly seems to spread its wings and move across my face and before you know it, I can feel Conrad's kiss all the way to the ends of my toes. And beyond that, I can feel the earth under me. I spread my arms out and I can almost follow the curve of it. I'm not on the outside anymore. I'm a part of Conrad, a part of Quentin, a part of the world. Yes I am. I'm a part of the world, lying here in the long green grass in this windy field, watching those old eighty-two-year-old brothers flying their aunt's airplane, pulling that banner back and forth across the sky, a banner that says BAILEY BROTHERS' HARDWARE, THERE WILL NEVER EVER BE BETTER.

chapter 28

About a week later Quentin Duster and I are walking along the road toward the old house. I'm heading over there with the little wounded bird in the shoebox. Granddaddy says to take it back where it was when we found it, now that it's time to let her go. Conrad isn't with us this afternoon because he has to help his mama get ready for a craft show over in Roanoke. If they sell two hundred fifty clothespin angels, Conrad's gonna get to spend the night at the Route 81 Howard Johnson's and he's gonna spend the whole time there lying in the swimming pool.

Quentin has found a tin can on the ground and he's kicking it along, keeping it on the road.

"Jessie Lou," he says, "what did you go to that stupid dance with Conrad for? He's just an old smelly sock, as far as I can see."

"He asked me, Quentin. I went 'cause he invited me," I say.

"Would you have gone with me, if I'd been in the sixth grade and I asked you?" he says, giving up on the tin can and knocking it away into the ferns.

"'Course I would have, Quentin Duster. I wouldn't have let a little old feller like yourself be lonesome with nobody to dance with. I would have danced the night away with you."

"Good," says Quentin, "'cause I wouldn't give you two cents for that old smelly sock you went with."

"Quentin, I thought you liked Conrad," I say. "Thought you got his autograph."

"I did, but then when you went to the dance with him, I sold his autograph to Moon n' Stars's little sister for two dollars. Couldn't stand the sight of it after that. Whole reason I came up to be friends with Conrad in the first place was 'cause I was afraid he'd take you away from me. I've liked you since third grade."

I look over at Quentin standing there all quivery and nervous and proud of himself at the same time. And I feel kind of warm inside and surprised too, like someone just gave me a little wrapped-up present that I didn't expect. "You know what we are, Quentin Duster, you and me and Conrad?" I say.

"What?" says Quentin.

"We're deep down friends, and as far as I'm concerned that's about better than anything."

"Oh," says Quentin, getting a nice little smile on his face.

"On the other hand," I say, breaking into a run, "if you want *my* autograph, it's gonna cost you five dollars."

I keep on running till I get to the top of the hill. I look back and see I'm way ahead of Quentin. Finally he gives up and I can see him back there on the road fiddling with his cousin's Discman, putting on headphones and singing along to himself.

I walk into Vera Bailey's yard. The grass is tall and deep green. Her silvery wooden house looks sorrowful and all alone in an ocean of waving grass. I sit on the porch in an old broken chair rocking back and forth. I hold the box with the little bird on my lap. My granddaddy did a nice job getting this bird all better. It is in there fluttering inside the box. I pull back the cloth cover ever so slightly and I take a peek. I've been help-ing to feed her for almost a week, and I think by the way that bird is moving around that she might be ready to go.

A tiny hummingbird is buzzing around a stand of newly opened peonies along the porch. I wonder if Vera Bailey planted those peonies. I think about her getting up in the morning and going out to her little barnstormer and taking an early morning ride over the fields here. I wonder what it feels like to see your house and your town and your school from the sky. It must give you a whole new way of thinking about things. I know Vera Bailey, being one of the Ninety-Nines, trained a lot of pilots. And I also know from looking up stuff on the computer that she was drop-ping supplies overseas for some troops during the war when her plane disappeared. She never came back, or at least she hasn't yet, and this little old house and her little 1930s barnstormer must have been sitting here waiting for her all these years.

I don't know if I would ever want to fly a plane myself, but I guess sometimes writing a poem feels something like flying. I sit here watching the hummingbird darting around Vera Bailey's flowers. I can see Quentin up on the road in the distance singing to himself. I guess the time has come. I can feel it all through me.

I look around at the grass and the sky and the sun. Then I open the screened top of the box and the little bird jumps to the edge of it, not realizing she's no longer captive. She sits there twittering for a moment and then suddenly she takes off into the air with a loud chirp and she flies across the yard and then circles around and heads over the field. Watching her, I can almost hear a country song playing in my head about a bird with a broken wing getting healed. I can hear Granddaddy making jokes about it, calling it cornball country, but I think I might write it down anyway. I might write the words to the song, the lyrics, and they might go something like this:

> *That bird was gonna fly higher and higher*
> *And nobody was going to stop her anymore*
> *Not now, not tomorrow, not ever again.*

epilogue

Things went along more or less at a normal pace after that. We had the sixth-grade graduation outdoors in the softball field behind the school. The fold-up chairs for the ceremony were supplied by Discount Beverage where Mama works. It threatened to rain all morning as we sat there listening to the principal's speech and then by the end of the ceremony, the sun was shining and Mrs. Duster was shining 'cause she made the right call. (The big question being, was it going to rain? Should the ceremony be held in the gym or on the softball field?)

When Mrs. Duster got up to hand out the diplomas, she gave a little talk about our future and how it lay before us like a great undiscovered wilderness and how we would each be like Lewis and Clark finding our own way. Then Quentin Duster, wearing a nice little suit and necktie, came up and presented Mrs. Duster with a bouquet of gladiolas from our whole class. Quentin had gotten the position by way of votes, which goes to show how things change around here.

Granddaddy and Mama sat up in the front row, and I just about died of embarrassment 'cause Granddaddy had tears rolling down his cheeks through the whole thing. We were wearing graduating gowns, which a lot of schools don't use at the sixth-grade level, but our school board pushed for it and we got them.

Each one of us had to walk up onstage and receive our sixth-grade diploma. When Conrad's name was called, he made his way up there smooth and easy, walking a perfect straight line. The crowd just went crazy clapping and calling out his name. And I felt glad for him, glad in my heart, because popularity suited Conrad and yet it seemed to roll off him like water, as if he knew what it was all about. When it was my turn to go up there, people cheered a little bit for me too, but I think it was ninety percent Granddaddy. I could hear his voice loud and clear, and

I felt proud and tearful and full of joy knowing he was cheering me on.

Even though Conrad and I and Quentin had been down in the field with the Bailey brothers' plane and not at the Big Box Home and Hardware celebration at the shopping mall, we heard that during the ceremony the Big Box Home and Hardware balloon truck, as it floated in the sky above, had popped and fizzled just at the height of one of the executive's speeches. It popped, making a lot of noise, and then it simply sailed down into the field nearby and landed there, looking like a great big washed-up rag.

The police came around to my house later that week asking a lot of questions about the destruction of the Big Box balloon truck. They asked if we had any idea who might have done it. "Quite frankly, somebody must have damaged that balloon before it even got up in the sky, like they did it on purpose. You know we found footprints on the side of that balloon that were bigger than seems humanly possible," said the policeman, taking off his hat and scratching the top of his head. "I mean, it was spooky." They walked through the kitchen asking Granddaddy all kinds of questions. (Mama was at work by then.) Granddaddy didn't really have any answers for them. All he could say was he was at church where everybody was supposed to be on a Sunday morning when all that nonsense went on.

I was lying on the couch in the living room at the time. I was watching TV and I never took my eyes off that show. And the officer never even thought to ask me anything. After all, I was just a kid and what do kids know anyway?

About our discovery reports, Conrad and I left Quentin Duster to write the story about finding the plane and Tiny Bailey in the woods. By the end of the year, Conrad and I had made other discoveries that we chose to write about instead. Quentin wrote his discovery report during study hall, spending all of one hour on the written part, and what I saw of it looked pretty dumb.

I do not know what Conrad's discovery paper was about. But I do know that the teacher was very pleased with it. She called it "a personal discovery about human nature," and she had nothing but praise for whatever it was Conrad had written.

For my part I chose to write about discovering that the abandoned house that I loved, where I spent time, where I did all my thinking and writing of my poems, turned out to belong to one of the first ninety-nine women airplane pilots in our country, one of the flying Ninety-Nines. I wrote in my report that I had always felt a kind of kinship with whoever had lived in that house and that I hoped I could grow up to be something like Vera Bailey. I wrote that she was for me kind of an unseen guide, like Sacagawea, or almost like a secret mother to me, someone who might be more like me than my own mama.

My sister Melinda and I became friends that spring through all that happened, and we spent the summer going together to all the Martha Nottingham Cake Mix parties. Melinda did all the bookkeeping and I did all the presenting and Mama didn't have to do anything except sit there watching everybody throwing orders at us.

But change was in the air. You could feel it all that summer when the wind went through the poplar trees along the river. You could hear it in the red-winged blackbirds calling in the long grassy fields around our house and in the crows cawing high up in the tops of the elm trees. Yes, things were changing.

By the end of the summer Bailey's Hardware closed its doors for good. Nobody came in and bought anything for most of the summer except for Granddaddy. He spent all kinds of money on things we didn't need and he stored all the stuff in a closet, till Mama found out about it and put an end to it.

Conrad and I went into Bailey's Hardware one afternoon, on one of the last days before they closed. A lot of the things were already boxed up and taken away. There weren't any bins of nails. The lights were bright. The store didn't have that dark oily mysterious smell, that smell that meant plans for summer projects, plans for painting an old fence, plans for wallpapering a back room with a big washtub full of sweet-smelling paste. Most everything was cleared away, making room for the bank that was taking its place, a bank with an automatic teller with a drive-through window where you wouldn't even have to get out of your car to do your banking.

Conrad and I were poking around at the back of

the store where Fred Bailey was throwing things out in big Dumpsters. Conrad was looking around and noticed one of the Dumpsters was filled to the brim with old tulip bulbs, five thousand at least. "Those are no good. They're dried out," said Fred Bailey. "I had to throw them all away. I bought too many of them. I can't sell them 'cause they're old and won't grow."

"Mind if we take them?" said Conrad.

"Be my guest," said Fred Bailey, "but I assure you they won't grow."

Conrad and Quentin and I spent a whole day hauling those tulip bulbs away in a wagon, and we got it into our minds to plant those tulip bulbs just for the heck of it in the field across the road from the old house.

Conrad and Quentin and I spent two weeks planting those five thousand bulbs. We used a pick and we drove a little hole and stuck in a bulb. Made a little hole, put in a bulb. Little hole, then a bulb, till we had tucked all five thousand of them into the ground. And then we forgot about it.

There were other things going on. Seventh grade was starting that fall and we had to learn how to change classes every hour when the bell rang. During that year

I grew taller just like a long-legged colt, my mama said. My hair grew down to my shoulders. Mama had to buy me a whole new wardrobe.

Just after Christmas, Melinda showed Granddaddy my poems and he insisted I send some in to the *Shenandoah Gazette,* which I did, and at the end of seventh grade, I had three poems printed in the paper with my name on them.

I think it was the week Granddaddy's senior citizens' bowling team made it to the state level that Frank Bailey landed a job at Big Box Home and Hardware in the fishing department. Granddaddy went over to visit him there now and again. Then they could often be seen together driving the forklift down the wide aisles at high speed, screeching around corners with great precision, coming close to huge piles of boxes but never knocking them over. "Your granddaddy capitulates," said Mama to me one day. "He adjusts. He's a survivor. He'll probably outlive us all, Jessie Lou," she said, wiping the table clean one more time.

Near the end of seventh grade in the spring, Conrad and I took a walk over the road along the Cabanash River toward Bailey's field. We could see the old house as we came to the peak in the hill, the silvery lonely-looking house with the wind hovering all around it.

"My granddaddy says in spite of it all, life is still something beautiful," I said.

"Guess he's right about that," said Conrad, smiling at me.

Then we looked over toward the field across the road. We hadn't thought about it till now. We just plain forgot about it. But then we started running. We ran and we ran and we ran, till we got to the field along the road. There we saw five thousand green shoots and buds coming up all over the field. Every tulip was going to bloom.

And not more than one week later, they did indeed bloom. That field was an enormous brilliant carpet of bright red tulips, a carpet that stretched from the rolling high rise all the way to the edge of the woods. Five thousand flowers blooming. A whole field of blazing bright red tulips.